A Hi

A Hidden Life and Other Poems

by George MacDonald

CONTENTS.

A HIDDEN LIFE THE HOMELESS GHOST ABU MIDJAN AN OLD STORY A BOOK OP DREAMS TO AURELIO SAFFI SONNET A MEMORIAL OF AFRICA A GIFT THE MAN OF SONGS BETTER THINGS THE JOURNEY PRAYER REST TO A.J. SCOTT LIGHT TO A.J. SCOTT WERE I A SKILFUL PAINTER IF I WERE A MONK, AND THOU WERT A NUN BLESSED ARE THE MEEK, FOR THEY SHALL INHERIT THE EARTH THE HILLS I KNOW WHAT BEAUTY IS I WOULD I WERE A CHILD THE LOST SOUL A DREAM WITHIN A DREAM AFTER AN OLD LEGEND THE TREE'S PRAYER A STORY OF THE SEA SHORE MY HEART O DO NOT LEAVE ME THE HOLY SNOWDROPS TO MY SISTER O THOU OF LITTLE FAITH LONGING A BOY'S GRIEF THE CHILD-MOTHER LOVE'S ORDEAL A PRAYER FOR THE PAST FAR AND NEAR MY ROOM SYMPATHY LITTLE ELFIE THE THANK OFFERING THE BURNT OFFERING FOUR SONNETS SONNET EIGHTEEN SONNETS DEATH AND BIRTH

EARLY POEMS.
LONGING MY EYES MAKE PICTURES DEATH LESSONS FOR A CHILD HOPE DEFERRED THE DEATH OF THE OLD YEAR A SONG IN A DREAM A THANKSGIVING

THE GOSPEL WOMEN.

THE MOTHER MARY THE WOMAN THAT CRIED IN THE CROWD THE MOTHER OF ZEBEDEE'S CHILDREN THE SYROPHENICIAN WOMAN THE WIDOW OF NAIN THE WOMAN WHOM SATAN HAD BOUND THE WOMAN WHO CAME BEHIND HIM IN THE CROWD THE WIDOW WITH THE TWO MITES THE WOMEN WHO MINISTERED UNTO HIM PILATE'S WIFE THE WOMAN OF SAMARIA MART MAGDALENE THE WOMAN IN THE TEMPLE MARTHA MARY THE WOMAN THAT WAS A SINNER
POEMS.

A HIDDEN LIFE.

   Proudly the youth, by manhood sudden crowned,
Went walking by his horses to the plough,
For the first time that morn. No soldier gay
Feels at his side the throb of the gold hilt
(Knowing the blue blade hides within its sheath,
As lightning in the cloud) with more delight,
When first he belts it on, than he that day
Heard still the clank of the plough-chains against
The horses' harnessed sides, as to the field
They went to make it fruitful. O'er the hill
The sun looked down, baptizing him for toil.
   A farmer's son he was, and grandson too;
Yea, his great-grandsire had possessed these fields.
Tradition said they had been tilled by men
Who bore the name long centuries ago,
And married wives, and reared a stalwart race,
And died, and went where all had followed them,
Save one old man, his daughter, and the youth
Who ploughs in pride, nor ever doubts his toil;
And death is far from him this sunny morn.
Why should we think of death when life is high?
The earth laughs all the day, and sleeps all night.
Earth, give us food, and, after that, a grave;
For both are good, each better in its time.
   The youth knew little; but he read old tales
Of Scotland's warriors, till his blood ran swift
As charging knights upon their death career.
And then he chanted old tunes, till the blood
Was charmed back into its fountain-well,
And tears arose instead. And Robert's songs,
Which ever flow in noises like his name,
Rose from him in the fields beside the kine,
And met the sky-lark's rain from out the clouds.
As yet he sang only as sing the birds,
From gladness simply, or, he knew not why.
The earth was fair—he knew not it was fair;
And he so glad—he knew not he was glad:
He walked as in a twilight of the sense,
Which this one day shall turn to tender light.
   For, ere the sun had cleared the feathery tops
Of the fir-thicket on the eastward hill,
His horses leaned and laboured. His great hands

Held both the reins and plough-stilts: he was proud;
Proud with a ploughman's pride; nobler, may be,
Than statesman's, ay, or poet's pride sometimes,
For little praise would come that he ploughed well,
And yet he did it well; proud of his work,
And not of what would follow. With sure eye,
He saw the horses keep the arrow-track;
He saw the swift share cut the measured sod;
He saw the furrow folding to the right,
Ready with nimble foot to aid at need.
And there the slain sod lay, patient for grain,
Turning its secrets upward to the sun,
And hiding in a grave green sun-born grass,
And daisies clipped in carmine: all must die,
That others live, and they arise again.
   Then when the sun had clomb to his decline,
And seemed to rest, before his slow descent,
Upon the keystone of his airy bridge,
They rested likewise, half-tired man and horse,
And homeward went for food and courage new;
Whereby refreshed, they turned again to toil,
And lived in labour all the afternoon.
Till, in the gloaming, once again the plough
Lay like a stranded bark upon the lea;
And home with hanging neck the horses went,
Walking beside their master, force by will.
Then through the deepening shades a vision came.
   It was a lady mounted on a horse,
A slender girl upon a mighty steed,
That bore her with the pride horses must feel
When they submit to women. Home she went,
Alone, or else the groom lagged far behind.
But, as she passed, some faithless belt gave way;
The saddle slipped, the horse stopped, and the girl
Stood on her feet, still holding fast the reins.
   Three paces bore him bounding to her side;
Her radiant beauty almost fixed him there;
But with main force, as one that gripes with fear,
He threw the fascination off, and saw
The work before him. Soon his hand and knife
Replaced the saddle firmer than before
Upon the gentle horse; and then he turned
To mount the maiden. But bewilderment
A moment lasted; for he knew not how,
With stirrup-hand and steady arm, to throne,
Elastic, on her steed, the ascending maid:

A moment only; for while yet she thanked,
Nor yet had time to teach her further will,
Around her waist he put his brawny hands,
That almost zoned her round; and like a child
Lifting her high, he set her on the horse;
Whence like a risen moon she smiled on him,
Nor turned away, although a radiant blush
Shone in her cheek, and shadowed in her eyes.
But he was never sure if from her heart
Or from the rosy sunset came the flush.
Again she thanked him, while again he stood
Bewildered in her beauty. Not a word
Answered her words that flowed, folded in tones
Round which dissolving lambent music played,
Like dropping water in a silver cup;
Till, round the shoulder of the neighbouring hill,
Sudden she disappeared. And he awoke,
And called himself hard names, and turned and went
After his horses, bending too his head.
   Ah God! when Beauty passes by the door,
Although she ne'er came in, the house grows bare.
Shut, shut the door; there's nothing in the house.
Why seems it always that it should be ours?
A secret lies behind which Thou dost know,
And I can partly guess.
            But think not then,
The holder of the plough had many sighs
Upon his bed that night; or other dreams
Than pleasant rose upon his view in sleep,
Within the magic crystal of the soul;
Nor that the airy castles of his brain
Had less foundation than the air admits.
But read my simple tale, scarce worth the name;
And answer, if he gained not from the fair
Beauty's best gift; and proved her not, in sooth,
An angel vision from a higher world.
   Not much of her I tell. Her changeful life
Where part the waters on the mountain ridge,
Flowed down the other side apart from his.
Her tale hath wiled deep sighs on summer eves,
Where in the ancient mysteries of woods
Walketh a man who worships womanhood.
Soon was she orphaned of such parent-haunts;
Surrounded with dead glitter, not the shine
Of leaves in wind and sunlight; while the youth
Breathed on, as if a constant breaking dawn

Sent forth the new-born wind upon his brow;
And knew the morning light was climbing up
The further hill-side—morning light, which most,
They say, reveals the inner hues of earth.
Now she was such as God had made her, ere
The world had tried to spoil her; tried, I say,
And half-succeeded, failing utterly.
Fair was she, frank, and innocent as a child
That stares you in the eyes; fearless of ill,
Because she knew it not; and brave withal,
Because she drank the draught that maketh strong,
The charmed country air. Her father's house—
A Scottish laird was he, of ancient name—
Stood only two miles off amid the hills;
But though she often passed alone as now,
The youth had never seen her face before,
And might not twice. Yet was not once enough?
It left him not. She, as the harvest moon
That goeth on her way, and knoweth not
The fields of grain whose ripening ears she fills
With wealth of life and human joyfulness,
Went on, and knew not of the influence
She left behind; yea, never thought of him;
Save at those times when, all at once, old scenes
Return uncalled, with wonder that they come,
Amidst far other thoughts and other cares;
Sinking again into their ancient graves,
Till some far-whispered necromantic spell
Loose them once more to wander for a space.
   Again I say, no fond romance of love,
No argument of possibilities,
If he were some one, and she claimed his aid,
Turned his clear brain into a nest of dreams.
As soon he had sat down and twisted cords
To snare, and carry home for daylight use,
Some woman-angel, wandering half-seen
On moonlight wings, o'er withered autumn fields.
But when he rose next morn, and went abroad,
(The exultation of his new-found rank
Already settling into dignity,)
He found the earth was beautiful. The sky,
Which shone with expectation of the sun,
Somehow, he knew not how, was like her face.
He grieved almost to plough the daisies down;
Something they shared in common with that smile
Wherewith she crowned his manhood; and they fell

Bent in the furrow, sometimes, with their heads
Just out imploringly. A hedgehog ran
With tangled mesh of bristling spikes, and face
Helplessly innocent, across the field:
He let it run, and blessed it as it ran.
At noon returning, something drew his feet
Into the barn. Entering, he gazed and stood.
Through the rent roof alighting, one sunbeam,
Blazing upon the straw one golden spot,
Dulled all the yellow heap, and sank far down,
Like flame inverted, through the loose-piled mound,
Crossing the splendour with the shadow-straws,
In lines innumerable. 'Twas so bright,
The eye was cheated with a spectral smoke
That rose as from a fire. He never knew,
Before, how beautiful the sunlight was;
Though he had seen it in the grassy fields,
And on the river, and the ripening corn,
A thousand times. He threw him on the heap,
And gazing down into the glory-gulf,
Dreamed as a boy half-sleeping by the fire;
And dreaming rose, and got his horses out.
   God, and not woman, is the heart of all.
But she, as priestess of the visible earth,
Holding the key, herself most beautiful,
Had come to him, and flung the portals wide.
He entered in: each beauty was a glass
That gleamed the woman back upon his view.
   Already in these hours his growing soul
Put forth the white tip of a floral bud,
Ere long to be a crown-like, shadowy flower.
For, by his songs, and joy in ancient tales,
He showed the seed lay hidden in his heart,
A safe sure treasure, hidden even from him,
And notwithstanding mellowing all his spring;
Until, like sunshine with its genial power,
Came the fair maiden's face: the seed awoke.
I need not follow him through many days;
Nor tell the joys that rose around his path,
Ministering pleasure for his labour's meed;
Nor how each morning was a boon to him;
Nor how the wind, with nature's kisses fraught,
Flowed inward to his soul; nor how the flowers
Asserted each an individual life,
A separate being, for and in his thought;
Nor how the stormy days that intervened

Called forth his strength, and songs that quelled their force;
Nor how in winter-time, when thick the snow
Armed the sad fields from gnawing of the frost,
And the low sun but skirted his far realms,
And sank in early night, he took his place
Beside the fire; and by the feeble lamp
Head book on book; and lived in other lives,
And other needs, and other climes than his;
And added other beings thus to his.
But I must tell that love of knowledge grew
Within him to a passion and a power;
Till, through the night (all dark, except the moon
Shone frosty o'er the lea, or the white snow
Gave back all motes of light that else had sunk
Into the thirsty earth) he bent his way
Over the moors to where the little town
Lay gathered in the hollow. There the man
Who taught the children all the shortened day,
Taught other scholars in the long fore-night;
And youths who in the shop, or in the barn,
Or at the loom, had done their needful work,
Came to his schoolroom in the murky night,
And found the fire aglow, the candles lit,
And the good master waiting for his men.
Here mathematics wiled him to their heights;
And strange consent of lines to form and law
Made Euclid like a great romance of truth.
The master saw with wonder how the youth
All eagerly devoured the offered food,
And straightway longed to lead him; with that hope
Of sympathy which urges him that knows
To multiply great knowledge by its gift;
That so two souls ere long may see one truth,
And, turning, see each others' faces shine.
So he proposed the classics; and the youth
Caught at the offer; and for many a night,
When others lay and lost themselves in sleep,
He groped his way with lexicon and rule,
Through ancient deeds embalmed in Latin old,
Or poet-woods alive with gracious forms;
Wherein his knowledge of the English tongue
(Through reading many books) much aided him—
For the soul's language is the same in all.
At length his progress, through the master's word,
Proud of his pupil, reached the father's ears.
Great joy arose within him, and he vowed,

If caring, sparing would accomplish it,
He should to college, and should have his fill
Of that same learning.
                  So to school he went,
Instead of to the plough; and ere a year,
He wore the scarlet gown with the close sleeves.
  Awkward at first, but with a dignity
That soon found fit embodiment in speech
And gesture and address, he made his way,
Not seeking it, to the respect of youths,
In whom respect is of the rarer gifts.
Likewise by the consent of accidents,
More than his worth, society, so called,
In that great northern city, to its rooms
Invited him. He entered. Dazzled first,
Not only by the brilliance of the show,
In lights and mirrors, gems, and crowded eyes;
But by the surface lights of many minds
Cut like rose-diamonds into many planes,
Which, catching up the wandering rays of fact,
Reflected, coloured, tossed them here and there,
In varied brilliance, as if quite new-born
From out the centre, not from off the face—
Dazzled at first, I say, he soon began
To see how little thought could sparkle well,
And turn him, even in the midst of talk,
Back to the silence of his homely toils.
Around him still and ever hung an air
Born of the fields, and plough, and cart, and scythe;
A kind of clumsy grace, in which gay girls
Saw but the clumsiness; while those with light,
Instead of glitter, in their quiet eyes,
Saw the grace too; yea, sometimes, when he talked,
Saw the grace only; and began at last,
As he sought none, to seek him in the crowd
(After a maiden fashion), that they might
Hear him dress thoughts, not pay poor compliments.
Yet seldom thus was he seduced from toil;
Or if one eve his windows showed no light,
The next, they faintly gleamed in candle-shine,
Till far into the morning. And he won
Honours among the first, each session's close.
  And if increased familiarity
With open forms of ill, not to be shunned
Where youths of all kinds meet, endangered there
A mind more willing to be pure than most—

Oft when the broad rich humour of a jest,
Did, with its breezy force, make radiant way
For pestilential vapours following—
Arose within his sudden silent mind,
The maiden face that smiled and blushed on him;
That lady face, insphered beyond his earth,
Yet visible to him as any star
That shines unwavering. I cannot tell
In words the tenderness that glowed across
His bosom—burned it clean in will and thought;
"Shall that sweet face be blown by laughter rude
Out of the soul where it has deigned to come,
But will not stay what maidens may not hear?"
He almost wept for shame, that those two thoughts
Should ever look each other in the face,
Meeting in *his* house. Thus he made to her,
For love, an offering of purity.
   And if the homage that he sometimes found,
New to the country lad, conveyed in smiles,
Assents, and silent listenings when he spoke,
Threatened yet more his life's simplicity;
An antidote of nature ever came,
Even nature's self. For, in the summer months,
His former haunts and boyhood's circumstance
Received him back within old influences.
And he, too noble to despise the past,
Too proud to be ashamed of manhood's toil,
Too wise to fancy that a gulf lay wide
Betwixt the labouring hand and thinking brain,
Or that a workman was no gentleman,
Because a workman, clothed himself again
In his old garments, took the hoe or spade,
Or sowing sheet, or covered in the grain,
Smoothing with harrows what the plough had ridged.
With ever fresher joy he hailed the fields,
Returning still with larger powers of sight:
Each time he knew them better than before,
And yet their sweetest aspect was the old.
His labour kept him true to life and fact,
Casting out worldly judgments, false desires,
And vain distinctions. Ever, at his toil,
New thoughts arose; which, when still night awoke,
He ever sought, like stars, with instruments;
By science, or by wise philosophy,
Bridging the gulf between them and the known;
And thus preparing for the coming months,

When in the time of snow, old Scotland's sons
Reap wisdom in the silence of the year.
   His sire was proud of him; and, most of all,
Because his learning did not make him proud.
A wise man builds not much upon his lore.
The neighbours asked what he would make his son.
"I'll make a man of him," the old man said;
"And for the rest, just what he likes himself.
But as he is my only son, I think
He'll keep the old farm joined to the old name;
And I shall go to the churchyard content,
Leaving my name amongst my fellow men,
As safe, thank God, as if I bore it still."
But sons are older than their sires full oft
In the new world that cometh after this.
   So four years long his life went to and fro
Betwixt the scarlet gown and rough blue coat;
The garret study and the wide-floored barn;
The wintry city, and the sunny fields.
In each his quiet mind was well content,
Because he was himself, where'er he was.
   Not in one channel flowed his seeking thoughts;
To no profession did he ardent turn:
He knew his father's wish—it was his own.
"Why should a man," he said, "when knowledge grows,
Leave therefore the old patriarchal life,
And seek distinction in the noise of men?"
And yet he turned his face on every side;
Went with the doctors to the lecture-room,
And saw the inner form of man laid bare;
Went with the chymists, where the skilful hand,
Revering laws higher than Nature's self,
Makes Nature do again, before our eyes,
And in a moment, what, in many years,
And in the veil of vastness and lone deeps,
She laboureth at alway, then best content
When man inquires into her secret ways;
Yea, turned his asking eye on every source
Whence knowledge floweth for the hearts of men,
Kneeling at some, and drinking freely there.
And at the end, when he had gained the right
To sit with covered head before the rank
Of black-gowned senators; and all these men
Were ready at a word to speed him on,
Proud of their pupil, towards any goal
Where he might fix his eye; he took his books,

What little of his gown and cap remained,
And, leaving with a sigh the ancient walls,
With the old stony crown, unchanging, grey,
Amidst the blandishments of airy Spring,
He sought for life the lone ancestral farm.
   With simple gladness met him on the road
His grey-haired father, elder brother now.
Few words were spoken, little welcome said,
But much was understood on either side.
If with a less delight he brought him home
Than he that met the prodigal returned,
Yet with more confidence, more certain joy;
And with the leaning pride that old men feel
In young strong arms that draw their might from them,
He led him to the house. His sister there,
Whose kisses were not many, but whose eyes
Were full of watchfulness and hovering love,
Set him beside the fire in the old place,
And heaped the table with best country fare.
And when the night grew deep, the father rose,
And led his son (who wondered why they went,
And in the darkness made a tortuous path
Through the corn-ricks) to an old loft, above
The stable where his horses rested still.
Entering, he saw some plan-pursuing hand
Had been at work. The father, leading on
Across the floor, heaped up with waiting grain,
Opened a door. An unexpected light
Flashed on them from a cheerful lamp and fire,
That burned alone, as in a fairy tale.
And lo! a little room, white-curtained bed,
An old arm-chair, bookshelves, and writing desk,
And some old prints of deep Virgilian woods,
And one a country churchyard, on the walls.
The young man stood and spoke not. The old love
Seeking and finding incarnation new,
Drew from his heart, as from the earth the sun,
Warm tears. The good, the fatherly old man,
Honouring in his son the simple needs
Which his own bounty had begot in him,
Thus gave him loneliness for silent thought,
A simple refuge he could call his own.
He grasped his hand and shook it; said good night,
And left him glad with love. Faintly beneath,
The horses stamped and drew the lengthening chain.

Three sliding years, with gently blending change,
Went round 'mid work of hands, and brain, and heart.
He laboured as before; though when he would,
With privilege, he took from hours of toil,
When nothing pressed; and read within his room,
Or wandered through the moorland to the hills;
There stood upon the apex of the world,
With a great altar-stone of rock beneath,
And looked into the wide abyss of blue
That roofed him round; and then, with steady foot,
Descended to the world, and worthy cares.
  And on the Sunday, father, daughter, son
Walked to the country church across the fields.
It was a little church, and plain, almost
To ugliness, yet lacking not a charm
To him who sat there when a little boy.
And the low mounds, with long grass waving on,
Were quite as solemn as great marble tombs.
And on the sunny afternoons, across
This well-sown field of death, when forth they came
With the last psalm still lingering in their hearts,
He looked, and wondered where the heap would rise
That rested on the arch of his dead breast.
But in the gloom and rain he turned aside,
And let the drops soak through the sinking clay—
What mattered it to him?
                        And as they walked
Together home, the father loved to hear
The new streams pouring from his son's clear well.
The old man clung not only to the old;
Nor bowed the young man only to the new;
Yet as they walked, full often he would say,
He liked not much what he had heard that morn.
He said, these men believed the past alone;
Honoured those Jewish times as they were Jews;
And had no ears for this poor needy hour,
That up and down the centuries doth go,
Like beggar boy that wanders through the streets,
With hand held out to any passer by;
And yet God made it, and its many cries.
  He used to say: "I take the work that comes
All ready to my hand. The lever set,
I grasp and heave withal. Or rather, I
Love where I live, and yield me to the will
That made the needs about me. It may be
I find them nearer to my need of work

Than any other choice. I would not choose
To lack a relish for the thing that God
Thinks worth. Among my own I will be good;
A helper to all those that look to me.
This farm is God's, as much as yonder town;
These men and maidens, kine and horses, his;
And need his laws of truth made rules of fact;
Or else the earth is not redeemed from ill."
He spoke not often; but he ruled and did.
No ill was suffered there by man or beast
That he could help; no creature fled from him;
And when he slew, 'twas with a sudden death,
Like God's benignant lightning. For he knew
That God doth make the beasts, and loves them well,
And they are sacred. Sprung from God as we,
They are our brethren in a lower kind;
And in their face he saw the human look.
They said: "Men look like different animals;"
But he: "The animals are like to men,
Some one, and some another." Cruelty,
He said, would need no other fiery hell,
Than that the ghosts of the sad beasts should come,
And crowding, silent, all their heads one way,
Stare the ill man to madness.
                    By degrees,
They knew not how, men trusted in him. When
He spoke, his word had all the force of deeds
That lay unsaid within him. To be good
Is more than holy words or definite acts;
Embodying itself unconsciously
In simple forms of human helpfulness,
And understanding of the need that prays.
And when he read the weary tales of crime,
And wretchedness, and white-faced children, sad
With hunger, and neglect, and cruel words,
He would walk sadly for an afternoon,
With head down-bent, and pondering footstep slow;
And to himself conclude: "The best I can
For the great world, is, just the best I can
For this my world. The influence will go
In widening circles to the darksome lanes
In London's self." When a philanthropist
Said pompously: "With your great gifts you ought
To work for the great world, not spend yourself
On common labours like a common man;"
He answered him: "The world is in God's hands.

This part he gives to me; for which my past,
Built up on loves inherited, hath made
Me fittest. Neither will He let me think
Primeval, godlike work too low to need,
For its perfection, manhood's noblest powers
And deepest knowledge, far beyond my gifts.
And for the crowds of men, in whom a soul
Cries through the windows of their hollow eyes
For bare humanity, and leave to grow,—
Would I could help them! But all crowds are made
Of individuals; and their grief, and pain,
And thirst, and hunger, all are of the one,
Not of the many. And the power that helps
Enters the individual, and extends
Thence in a thousand gentle influences
To other hearts. It is not made one's own
By laying hold of an allotted share
Of general good divided faithfully.
Now here I labour whole upon the place
Where they have known me from my childhood up.
I know the individual man; and he
Knows me. If there is power in me to help,
It goeth forth beyond the present will,
Clothing itself in very common deeds
Of any humble day's necessity:
—I would not always consciously do good;
Not always feel a helper of the men,
Who make me full return for my poor deeds
(Which I *must* do for my own highest sake,
If I forgot my brethren for themselves)
By human trust, and confidence of eyes
That look me in the face, and hands that do
My work at will—'tis more than I deserve.
But in the city, with a few lame words,
And a few scanty handfuls of weak coin,
Misunderstood, or, at the best, unknown,
I should toil on, and seldom reach the mail.
And if I leave the thing that lieth next,
To go and do the thing that is afar,
I take the very strength out of my deed,
Seeking the needy not for pure need's sake."
Thus he. The world-wise schemer for the good
Held his poor peace, and left him to his way.
   What of the vision now? the vision fair
Sent forth to meet him, when at eve he went
Home from his first day's ploughing? Oft she passed

Slowly on horseback, in all kinds of dreams;
For much he dreamed, and loved his dreaming well.
Nor woke he from such dreams with vain regret;
But, saying, "I have seen that face once more,"
He smiled with his eyes, and rose to work.
Nor did he turn aside from other maids,
But loved the woman-faces and dear eyes;
And sometimes thought, "One day I wed a maid,
And make her mine;" but never came the maid,
Or never came the hour, that he might say,
"I wed this maid." And ever when he read
A tale of lofty aim, or when the page
Of history spoke of woman very fair,
Or wondrous good, her face arose, and stayed,
The face for ever of that storied page.

   Meantime how fared the lady? She had wed
One of those common men, who serve as ore
For the gold grains to lie in. Virgin gold
Lay hidden there—no richer was the dross.
She went to gay assemblies, not content;
For she had found no hearts, that, struck with hers,
Sounded one chord. She went, and danced, or sat
And listlessly conversed; or, if at home,
Read the new novel, wishing all the time
For something better; though she knew not what,
Or how to search for it.
                      What had she felt,
If, through the rhythmic motion of light forms,
A vision, had arisen; as when, of old,
The minstrel's art laid bare the seer's eye,
And showed him plenteous waters in the waste?
If she had seen her ploughman-lover go
With his great stride across some lonely field,
Beneath the dark blue vault, ablaze with stars,
And lift his full eyes to earth's radiant roof
In gladness that the roof was yet a floor
For other feet to tread, for his, one day?
Or the emerging vision might reveal
Him, in his room, with space-compelling mind,
Pursue, upon his slate, some planet's course;
Or read, and justify the poet's wrath,
Or wise man's slow conclusion; or, in dreams,
All gently bless her with a trembling voice
For that old smile, that withered nevermore,
That woke him, smiled him into what he is;
Or, kneeling, cry to God for better still.

Would those dark eyes have beamed with darker light?
Would that fair soul, all tired of emptiness,
Have risen from the couch of its unrest,
And looked to heaven again, again believed
In God's realities of life and fact?
Would not her soul have sung unto itself,
In secret joy too good for that vain throng:
"I have a friend, a ploughman, who is wise,
And knoweth God, and goodness, and fair faith;
Who needeth not the outward shows of things,
But worships the unconquerable truth:
And this man loveth me; I will be proud
And humble—would he love me if he knew?"
   In the third year, a heavy harvest fell,
Full filled, beneath the reaping-hook and scythe.
The men and maidens in the scorching heat
Held on their toil, lightened by song and jest;
Resting at mid-day, and from brimming bowl,
Drinking brown ale, and white abundant milk;
Until the last ear fell, and stubble stood
Where waved the forests of the murmuring corn;
And o'er the land rose piled the tent-like shocks,
As of an army resting in array
Of tent by tent, rank following on rank;
Waiting until the moon should have her will
Of ripening on the ears.
                And all went well.
The grain was fully ripe. The harvest carts
Went forth broad-platformed for the towering load,
With frequent passage 'twixt homeyard and field.
And half the oats already hid their tops,
Of countless spray-hung grains—their tops, by winds
Swayed oft, and ringing, rustling contact sweet;
Made heavy oft by slow-combining dews,
Or beaten earthward by the pelting rains;
Rising again in breezes to the sun,
And bearing all things till the perfect time—
Had hid, I say, this growth of sun and air
Within the darkness of the towering stack;
When in the north low billowy clouds appeared,
Blue-based, white-topped, at close of afternoon;
And in the west, dark masses, plashed with blue,
With outline vague of misty steep and dell,
Clomb o'er the hill-tops; there was thunder there.
The air was sultry. But the upper sky
Was clear and radiant.

           Downward went the sun;
Down low, behind the low and sullen clouds
That walled the west; and down below the hills
That lay beneath them hid. Uprose the moon,
And looked for silence in her moony fields,
But there she found it not. The staggering cart,
Like an o'erladen beast, crawled homeward still,
Returning light and low. The laugh broke yet,
That lightning of the soul, from cloudless skies,
Though not so frequent, now that labour passed
Its natural hour. Yet on the labour went,
Straining to beat the welkin-climbing toil
Of the huge rain-clouds, heavy with their floods.
Sleep, like enchantress old, soon sided with
The crawling clouds, and flung benumbing spells
On man and horse. The youth that guided home
The ponderous load of sheaves, higher than wont,
Daring the slumberous lightning, with a start
Awoke, by falling full against the wheel,
That circled slow after the sleepy horse.
Yet none would yield to soft-suggesting sleep,
Or leave the last few shocks; for the wild rain
Would catch thereby the skirts of Harvest-home,
And hold her lingering half-way in the storm.
   The scholar laboured with his men all night.
Not that he favoured quite this headlong race
With Nature. He would rather say: "The night
Is sent for sleep, we ought to sleep in it,
And leave the clouds to God. Not every storm
That climbeth heavenward, overwhelms the earth.
And if God wills, 'tis better as he wills;
What he takes from us never can be lost."
But the old farmer ordered; and the son
Went manful to the work, and held his peace.
    The last cart homeward went, oppressed with sheaves,
Just as a moist dawn blotted pale the east,
And the first drops fell, overfed with mist,
O'ergrown and helpless. Darker grew the morn.
Upstraining racks of clouds, tumultuous borne
Upon the turmoil of opposing winds,
Met in the zenith. And the silence ceased:
The lightning brake, and flooded all the earth,
And its great roar of billows followed it.
The deeper darkness drank the light again,
And lay unslaked. But ere the darkness came,
In the full revelation of the flash,

He saw, along the road, borne on a horse
Powerful and gentle, the sweet lady go,
Whom years agone he saw for evermore.
"Ah me!" he said; "my dreams are come for me,
Now they shall have their time." And home he went,
And slept and moaned, and woke, and raved, and wept.
Through all the net-drawn labyrinth of his brain
The fever raged, like pent internal fire.
His father soon was by him; and the hand
Of his one sister soothed him. Days went by.
As in a summer evening, after rain,
He woke to sweet quiescent consciousness;
Enfeebled much, but with a new-born life.
   As slow the weeks passed, he recovered strength;
And ere the winter came, seemed strong once more.
But the brown hue of health had not returned
On his thin face; although a keener fire
Burned in his larger eyes; and in his cheek
The mounting blood glowed radiant (summoning force,
Sometimes, unbidden) with a sunset red.
   Before its time, a biting frost set in;
And gnawed with fangs of cold his shrinking life;
And the disease so common to the north
Was born of outer cold and inner heat.
One morn his sister, entering, saw he slept;
But in his hand he held a handkerchief
Spotted with crimson. White with terror, she
Stood motionless and staring. Startled next
By her own pallor, when she raised her eyes,
Seen in the glass, she moved at last. He woke;
And seeing her dismay, said with a smile,
"Blood-red was evermore my favourite hue,
And see, I have it in me; that is all."
She shuddered; and he tried to jest no more;
And from that hour looked Death full in the face.
   When first he saw the red blood outward leap,
As if it sought again the fountain heart,
Whence it had flowed to fill the golden bowl;
No terror, but a wild excitement seized
His spirit; now the pondered mystery
Of the unseen would fling its portals wide,
And he would enter, one of the awful dead;
Whom men conceive as ghosts that fleet and pine,
Bereft of weight, and half their valued lives;—
But who, he knew, must live intenser life,
Having, through matter, all illumed with sense,

Flaming, like Horeb's bush, with present soul,
And by the contact with a thousand souls,
Each in the present glory of a shape,
Sucked so much honey from the flower o' the world,
And kept the gain, and cast the means aside;
And now all eye, all ear, all sense, perhaps;
Transformed, transfigured, yet the same life-power
That moulded first the visible to its use.
So, like a child he was, that waits the show,
While yet the panting lights restrained burn
At half height, and the theatre is full.
   But as the days went on, they brought sad hours,
When he would sit, his hands upon his knees,
Drooping, and longing for the wine of life.
Ah! now he learned what new necessities
Come when the outer sphere of life is riven,
And casts distorted shadows on the soul;
While the poor soul, not yet complete in God,
Cannot with inward light burn up the shades,
And laugh at seeming that is not the fact.
For God, who speaks to man on every side,
Sending his voices from the outer world,
Glorious in stars, and winds, and flowers, and waves,
And from the inner world of things unseen,
In hopes and thoughts and deep assurances,
Not seldom ceases outward speech awhile,
That the inner, isled in calm, may clearer sound;
Or, calling through dull storms, proclaim a rest,
One centre fixed amid conflicting spheres;
And thus the soul, calm in itself, become
Able to meet and cope with outward things,
Which else would overwhelm it utterly;
And that the soul, saying *I will the light*,
May, in its absence, yet grow light itself,
And man's will glow the present will of God,
Self-known, and yet divine.
                        Ah, gracious God!
Do with us what thou wilt, thou glorious heart!
Thou art the God of them that grow, no less
Than them that are; and so we trust in thee
For what we shall be, and in what we are.
   Yet in the frequent pauses of the light,
When fell the drizzling thaw, or flaky snow;
Or when the heaped-up ocean of still foam
Reposed upon the tranced earth, breathing low;
His soul was like a frozen lake beneath

The clear blue heaven, reflecting it so dim
That he could scarce believe there was a heaven;
And feared that beauty might be but a toy
Invented by himself in happier moods.
"For," said he, "if my mind can dim the fair,
Why should it not enhance the fairness too?"
But then the poor mind lay itself all dim,
And ruffled with the outer restlessness
Of striving death and life. And a tired man
May drop his eyelids on the visible world,
To whom no dreams, when fancy flieth free,
Will bring the sunny excellence of day;
Nor will his utmost force increase his sight.
'Tis easy to destroy, not so to make.
No keen invention lays the strata deep
Of ancient histories; or sweeps the sea
With purple shadows and blue breezes' tracks,
Or rosy memories of the down-gone sun.
And if God means no beauty in these shows,
But drops them, helpless shadows, from his sun,
Ah me, my heart! thou needst another God.
Oh! lack and doubt and fear can only come
Because of plenty, confidence, and love:
Without the mountain there were no abyss.
Our spirits, inward cast upon themselves,
Because the delicate ether, which doth make
The mediator with the outer world,
Is troubled and confused with stormy pain;
Not glad, because confined to shuttered rooms,
Which let the sound of slanting rain be heard,
But show no sparkling sunlight on the drops,
Or ancient rainbow dawning in the west;—
Cast on themselves, I say, nor finding there
The thing they need, because God has not come,
And, claiming all their Human his Divine,
Revealed himself in all their inward parts,
Go wandering up and down a dreary house.
Thus reasoned he. Yet up and down the house
He wandered moaning. Till his soul and frame,
In painful rest compelled, full oft lay still,
And suffered only. Then all suddenly
A light would break from forth an inward well—
God shone within him, and the sun arose.
And to its windows went the soul and looked:—
Lo! o'er the bosom of the outspread earth
Flowed the first waves of sunrise, rippling on.

Much gathered he of patient faith from off
These gloomy heaths, this land of mountains dark,
By moonlight only, like the sorcerer's weeds;
As testify these written lines of his
Found on his table, when his empty chair
Stood by the wall, with yet a history
Clinging around it for the old man's eyes.
    I am weary, and something lonely;
      And can only think, think.
  I If there were some water only,
    That a spirit might drink, drink!
      And rise
      With light in the eyes,
    And a crown of hope on the brow;
      And walk in outgoing gladness,—
      Not sit in an inward sadness—
        As now!
    But, Lord, thy child will be sad,
      As sad as it pleaseth thee;
  Will sit, not needing to be glad,
    Till thou bid sadness flee;
      And drawing near
      With a simple cheer,
      Speak one true word to me.
  Another song in a low minor key
From awful holy calm, as this from grief,
I weave, a silken flower, into my web,
That goes straight on, with simply crossing lines,
Floating few colours upward to the sight.
    Ah, holy midnight of the soul,
      When stars alone are high;
      When winds are dead, or at their goal,
        And sea-waves only sigh!
      Ambition faints from out the will;
        Asleep sad longing lies;
    All hope of good, all fear of ill,
      All need of action dies;
      Because God is; and claims the life
        He kindled in thy brain;
      And thou in Him, rapt far from strife,
        Diest and liv'st again.
  It was a changed and wintry time to him;
But visited by April airs and scents,
That came with sudden presence, unforetold;
As brushed from off the outer spheres of spring
In the new singing world, by winds of sighs,

That wandering swept across the glad *To be*.
Strange longings that he never knew till now,
A sense of want, yea of an infinite need,
Cried out within him—rather moaned than cried.
And he would sit a silent hour and gaze
Upon the distant hills with dazzling snow
Upon their peaks, and thence, adown their sides,
Streaked vaporous, or starred in solid blue.
And then a shadowy sense arose in him,
As if behind those world-inclosing hills,
There sat a mighty woman, with a face
As calm as life, when its intensity
Pushes it nigh to death, waiting for him,
To make him grand for ever with a kiss,
And send him silent through the toning worlds.
   The father saw him waning. The proud sire
Beheld his pride go drooping in the cold
Down, down to the warm earth; and gave God thanks
That he was old. But evermore the son
Looked up and smiled as he had heard strange news,
Across the waste, of primrose-buds and flowers.
Then again to his father he would come
Seeking for comfort, as a troubled child,
And with the same child's hope of comfort there.
Sure there is one great Father in the heavens,
Since every word of good from fathers' lips
Falleth with such authority, although
They are but men as we: God speaks in them.
So this poor son who neared the unknown death,
Took comfort in his father's tenderness,
And made him strong to die. One day he came,
And said: "What think you, father, is it hard,
This dying?" "Well, my boy," he said, "We'll try
And make it easy with the present God.
But, as I judge, though more by hope than sight,
It seemeth harder to the lookers on,
Than him that dieth. It may be, each breath,
That they would call a gasp, seems unto him
A sigh of pleasure; or, at most, the sob
Wherewith the unclothed spirit, step by step,
Wades forth into the cool eternal sea.
I think, my boy, death has two sides to it,
One sunny, and one dark; as this round earth
Is every day half sunny and half dark.
We on the dark side call the mystery *death*;
They on the other, looking down in light,

Wait the glad birth, with other tears than ours."
"Be near me, father, when I die;" he said.
"I will, my boy, until a better sire
Takes your hand out of mine, and I shall say:
I give him back to thee; Oh! love him, God;
For he needs more than I can ever be.
And then, my son, mind and be near in turn,
When my time comes; you in the light beyond,
And knowing all about it; I all dark."
   And so the days went on, until the green
Shone through the snow in patches, very green:
For, though the snow was white, yet the green shone.
And hope of life awoke within his heart;
For the spring drew him, warm, soft, budding spring,
With promises. The father better knew.
God, give us heaven. Remember our poor hearts.
We never grasp the zenith of the time;
We find no spring, except in winter prayers.
   Now he, who strode a king across his fields,
Crept slowly through the breathings of the spring;
And sometimes wept in secret, that the earth,
Which dwelt so near his heart with all its suns,
And moons, and maidens, soon would lie afar
Across some unknown, sure-dividing waste.
Yet think not, though I fall upon the sad,
And lingering listen to the fainting tones,
Before I strike new chords that seize the old
And waft their essence up the music-stair—
Think not that he was always sad, nor dared
To look the blank unknown full in the void:
For he had hope in God, the growth of years,
Ponderings, and aspirations from a child,
And prayers and readings and repentances.
Something within him ever sought to come
At peace with something deeper in him still.
Some sounds sighed ever for a harmony
With other deeper, fainter tones, that still
Drew nearer from the unknown depths, wherein
The Individual goeth out in God,
And smoothed the discord ever as they grew.
Now he went back the way the music came,
Hoping some nearer sign of God at hand;
And, most of all, to see the very face
That in Judea once, at supper time,
Arose a heaven of tenderness above

The face of John, who leaned upon the breast
Soon to lie down in its last weariness.
   And as the spring went on, his budding life
Swelled up and budded towards the invisible,
Bursting the earthy mould wherein it lay.
He never thought of churchyards, as before,
When he was strong; but ever looked above,
Away from the green earth to the blue sky,
And thanked God that he died not in the cold.
"For," said he, "I would rather go abroad
When the sun shines, and birds are happy here.
For, though it may be we shall know no place,
But only mighty realms of making thought,
(Not living in creation any more,
But evermore creating our own worlds)
Yet still it seems as if I had to go
Into the sea of air that floats and heaves,
And swings its massy waves around our earth,
And may feel wet to the unclothed soul;
And I would rather go when it is full
Of light and blueness, than when grey and fog
Thicken it with the steams of the old earth.
Now in the first of summer I shall die;
Lying, mayhap, at sunset, sinking asleep,
And going with the light, and from the dark;
And when the earth is dark, they'll say: 'He is dead;'
But I shall say: 'Ah God! I live and love;
The earth is fair, but this is fairer still;
My dear ones, they were very dear; but now
The past is past; for they are dearer still.'
So I shall go, in starlight, it may be,
Or lapt in moonlight ecstasies, to seek
The heart of all, the man of all, my friend;
Whom I shall know my own beyond all loves,
Because he makes all loving true and deep;
And I live on him, in him, he in me."
   The weary days and nights had taught him much;
Had sent him, as a sick child creeps along,
Until he hides him in his mother's breast,
Seeking for God. For all he knew before
Seemed as he knew it not. He needed now
To feel God's arms around him hold him close,
Close to his heart, ere he could rest an hour.
And God was very good to him, he said.
   Ah God! we need the winter as the spring;
And thy poor children, knowing thy great heart,

And that thou bearest thy large share of grief,
Because thou lovest goodness more than joy
In them thou lovest,—so dost let them grieve,
Will cease to vex thee with their peevish cries,
Will look and smile, though they be sorrowful;
And not the less pray for thy help, when pain
Is overstrong, coming to thee for rest.
One day we praise thee for, without, the pain.
  One night, as oft, he lay and could not sleep.
His soul was like an empty darkened room,
Through which strange pictures pass from the outer world;
While regnant will lay passive and looked on.
But the eye-tube through which the shadows came
Was turned towards the past. One after one
Arose old scenes, old sorrows, old delights.
Ah God! how sad are all things that grow old;
Even the rose-leaves have a mournful scent,
And old brown letters are more sad than graves;
Old kisses lie about the founts of tears,
Like autumn leaves around the winter wells;
And yet they cannot die. A smile once smiled
Is to eternity a smile—no less;
And that which smiles and kisses, liveth still;
And thou canst do great wonders, Wonderful!
  At length, as ever in such vision-hours,
Came the bright maiden, riding the great horse.
And then at once the will sprang up awake,
And, like a necromantic sage, forbade
What came unbidden to depart at will.
So on that form he rested his sad thoughts,
Till he began to wonder what her lot;
How she had fared in spinning history
Into a psyche-cradle, where to die;
And then emerge—what butterfly? pure white,
With silver dust of feathers on its wings?
Or that dull red, seared with its ebon spots?
And then he thought: "I know some women fail,
And cease to be so very beautiful.
And I have heard men rave of certain eyes,
In which I could not rest a moment's space."
Straightway the fount of possibilities
Began to gurgle, under, in his soul.
Anon the lava-stream burst forth amain,
And glowed, and scorched, and blasted as it flowed.
For purest souls sometimes have direst fears,
In ghost-hours when the shadow of the earth

Is cast on half her children, from the sun
Who is afar and busy with the rest.
"If my high lady be but only such
As some men say of women—very pure
When dressed in white, and shining in men's eyes,
And with the wavings of great unborn wings
Around them in the aether of the souls,
Felt at the root where senses meet in one
Like dim-remembered airs and rhymes and hues;
But when alone, at best a common thing,
With earthward thoughts, and feet that are of earth!
Ah no—it cannot be! She is of God.
But then, fair things may perish; higher life
Gives deeper death; fair gifts make fouler faults:
Women themselves—I dare not think the rest.
And then they say that in her London world,
They have other laws and judgments than in ours."
And so the thoughts walked up and down his soul,
And found at last a spot wherein to rest,
Building a resolution for the day.
   But next day, and the next, he was too worn
With the unrest of this chaotic night—
As if a man had sprung to life before
The spirit of God moved on the waters' face,
And made his dwelling ready, who in pain,
Himself untuned, groaned for a harmony,
For order and for law around his life—
Too tired he was to do as he had planned.
But on the next, a genial south-born wind
Waved the blue air beneath the golden sun,
Bringing glad news of summer from the south.
Into his little room the bright rays shone,
And, darting through the busy blazing fire,
Turning it ghostly pale, slew it almost;
As the great sunshine of the further life
Quenches the glow of this, and giveth death.
He had lain gazing at the wondrous strife
And strange commingling of the sun and fire,
Like spiritual and vital energies,
Whereof the one doth bear the other first,
And then destroys it for a better birth;
And now he rose to help the failing fire,
Because the sunshine came not near enough
To do for both. And then he clothed himself,
And sat him down betwixt the sun and fire,
And got him ink and paper, and began

And wrote with earnest dying heart as thus.
"Lady, I owe thee much. Nay, do not look
To find my name; for though I write it here,
I date as from the churchyard, where I lie
Whilst thou art reading; and thou know'st me not.
I dare to write, because I am crowned by death
Thy equal. If my boldness should offend,
I, pure in my intent, hide with the ghosts,
Where thou wilt never meet me, until thou
Knowest that death, like God, doth make of one.
   "But pardon, lady. Ere I had begun,
My thoughts moved towards thee with a gentle flow
That bore a depth of waters. When I took
My pen to write, they rushed into a gulf,
Precipitate and foamy. Can it be,
That death who humbles all hath made me proud?
Lady, thy loveliness hath walked my brain,
As if I were thy heritage in sooth,
Bequeathed from sires beyond all story's reach.
For I have loved thee from afar, and long;
Joyous in having seen what lifted me,
By very power to see, above myself.
Thy beauty hath made beautiful my life;
Thy virtue made mine strong to be itself.
Thy form hath put on every changing dress
Of name, and circumstance, and history,
That so the life, dumb in the wondrous page
Recording woman's glory, might come forth
And be the living fact to longing eyes—
Thou, thou essential womanhood to me;
Afar as angels or the sainted dead,
Yet near as loveliness can haunt a man,
And taking any shape for every need.
   "Years, many years, have passed since the first time,
Which was the last, I saw thee. What have they
Made or unmade in thee? I ask myself.
O lovely in my memory! art thou
As lovely in thyself? Thy features then
Said what God made thee; art thou such indeed?
Forgive my boldness, lady; I am dead;
And dead men may cry loud, they make no noise.
   "I have a prayer to make thee—hear the dead.
Lady, for God's sake be as beautiful
As that white form that dwelleth in my heart;
Yea, better still, as that ideal Pure
That waketh in thee, when thou prayest God,

Or helpest thy poor neighbour. For myself
I pray. For if I die and find that she,
My woman-glory, lives in common air,
Is not so very radiant after all,
My sad face will afflict the calm-eyed ghosts,
Not used to see such rooted sadness there,
At least in fields where I may hope to walk
And find good company. Upon my knees
I could implore thee—justify my faith
In womanhood's white-handed nobleness,
And thee, its revelation unto me.
 "But I bethink me, lady. If thou turn
Thy thoughts upon thyself, for the great sake
Of purity and conscious whiteness' self,
Thou wilt but half succeed. The other half
Is to forget the first, and all thyself,
Quenching thy moonlight in the blaze of day;
Turning thy being full unto thy God;
Where shouldst thou quite forget the name of Truth,
Yet thou wouldst be a pure, twice holy child,
(Twice born of God, once of thy own pure will
Arising at the calling Father's voice,)
Doing the right with sweet unconsciousness;
Having God in thee, a completer soul,
Be sure, than thou alone; thou not the less
Complete in choice, and individual life,
Since that which sayeth *I*, doth call him *Sire*.
 "Lady, I die—the Father holds me up.
It is not much to thee that I should die;
(How should it be? for thou hast never looked
Deep in my eyes, as I once looked in thine)
But it is much that He doth hold me up.
 "I thank thee, lady, for a gentle look
Thou lettest fall upon me long ago.
The same sweet look be possible to thee
For evermore;—I bless thee with thine own,
And say farewell, and go into my grave—
Nay, nay, into the blue heaven of my hopes."
 Then came his name in full, and then the name
Of the green churchyard where he hoped to lie.
And then he laid him back, weary, and said:
"O God! I am only an attempt at life.
Sleep falls again ere I am full awake.
Life goeth from me in the morning hour.
I have seen nothing clearly; felt no thrill
Of pure emotion, save in dreams, wild dreams;

And, sometimes, when I looked right up to thee.
I have been proud of knowledge, when the flame
Of Truth, high Truth, but flickered in my soul.
Only at times, in lonely midnight hours,
When in my soul the stars came forth, and brought
New heights of silence, quelling all my sea,
Have I beheld clear truth, apart from form,
And known myself a living lonely thought,
Isled in the hyaline of Truth alway.
I have not reaped earth's harvest, O my God;
Have gathered but a few poor wayside flowers,
Harebells, red poppies, closing pimpernels—
All which thou hast invented, beautiful God,
To gather by the way, for comforting.
Have I aimed proudly, therefore aimed too low,
Striving for something visible in my thought,
And not the unseen thing hid far in thine?
Make me content to be a primrose-flower
Among thy nations; that the fair truth, hid
In the sweet primrose, enter into me,
And I rejoice, an individual soul,
Reflecting thee; as truly then divine,
As if I towered the angel of the sun.
All in the night, the glowing worm hath given
Me keener joy than a whole heaven of stars:
Thou camest in the worm more near me then.
Nor do I think, were I that green delight,
I'd change to be the shadowy evening star.
Ah, make me, Father, anything thou wilt,
So be thou will it; I am safe with thee.
I laugh exulting. Make me something, God;
Clear, sunny, veritable purity
Of high existence, in itself content,
And in the things that are besides itself,
And seeking for no measures. I have found
The good of earth, if I have found this death.
Now I am ready; take me when thou wilt."
  He laid the letter in his desk, with seal
And superscription. When his sister came,
He said, "You'll find a note there—afterwards—.
Take it yourself to the town, and let it go.
But do not see the name, my sister true—
I'll tell you all about it, when you come."
  And as the eve, through paler, darker shades,
Insensibly declines, and is no more,
The lordly day once more a memory,

So died he. In the hush of noon he died.
Through the low valley-fog he brake and climbed.
The sun shone on—why should he not shine on?
The summer noises rose o'er all the land.
The love of God lay warm on hill and plain.
'Tis well to die in summer.
                    When the breath,
After a long still pause, returned no more,
The old man sank upon his knees, and said:
"Father, I thank thee; it is over now;
And thou hast helped him well through this sore time.
So one by one we all come back to thee,
All sons and brothers, thanking thee who didst
Put of thy fatherhood in our poor hearts,
That, having children, we might guess thy love.
And at the last, find all loves one in thee."
And then he rose, and comforted the maid,
Who in her brother lost the pride of life,
Weeping as all her heaven were full of rain.
  When that which was so like him—so unlike—
Lay in the churchyard, and the green turf soon
Would grow together, healing up the wounds
Of the old Earth who took her share again,
The sister went to do his last request.
Then found she, with his other papers, this,—
A farewell song, in lowland Scottish tongue:—
    Greetna, father, that I'm gaein'.
    For fu' weel ye ken the gaet.
    I' the winter, corn ye're sawin'—
    I' the hairst, again ye hae't.
    I'm gaein' hame to see my mither—
    She'll be weel acquant or this,
    Sair we'll muse at ane anither,
    'Tween the auld word an' new kiss.
    Love, I'm doubtin', will be scanty
    Roun' ye baith, when I'm awa';
    But the kirk has happin' plenty
    Close aside me, for you twa.
    An' aboon, there's room for mony—
    'Twas na made for ane or twa;
    But it grew for a' an' ony
    Countin' love the best ava'.
    Here, aneath, I ca' ye father:
    Auld names we'll nor tyne nor spare;
    A' my sonship I maun gather,
    For the Son is King up there.

  Greetna, father, that I'm gaein';
   For ye ken fu' weel the gaet:
  Here, in winter, cast yer sawin'—
   There, in hairst, again ye hae't.
 What of the lady? Little more I know.
Not even if, when she had read the lines,
She rose in haste, and to her chamber went,
And shut the door; nor if, when she came forth,
A dawn of holier purpose shone across
The sadness of her brow; unto herself
Convicted; though the great world, knowing all,
Might call her pure as day—yea, truth itself.
Of these things I know nothing—only know
That on a warm autumnal afternoon,
When half-length shadows fell from mossy stones,
Darkening the green upon the grassy graves,
While the still church, like a said prayer, arose
White in the sunshine, silent as the graves,
Empty of souls, as is the tomb itself;
A little boy, who watched a cow near by
Gather her milk from alms of clover fields,
Flung over earthen dykes, or straying out
Beneath the gates upon the paths, beheld
All suddenly—he knew not how she came—
A lady, closely veiled, alone, and still,
Seated upon a grave. Long time she sat
And moved not, "greetin' sair," the boy did say;
"Just like my mither whan my father deed.
An' syne she rase, an' pu'd at something sma',
A glintin' gowan, or maybe a blade
O' the dead grass," and glided silent forth,
Over the low stone wall by two old steps,
And round the corner, and was seen no more.
The clang of hoofs and sound of carriage wheels
Arose and died upon the listener's ear.
 THE HOMELESS GHOST.
 Still flowed the music, flowed the wine.
  The youth in silence went;
Through naked streets, in cold moonshine,
  His homeward way he bent,
Where, on the city's seaward line,
  His lattice seaward leant.
 He knew not why he left the throng,
  But that he could not rest;
That something pained him in the song,
  And mocked him in the jest;

And a cold moon-glitter lay along
  One lovely lady's breast.
   He sat him down with solemn book
   His sadness to beguile;
A skull from off its bracket-nook
  Threw him a lipless smile;
But its awful, laughter-mocking look,
  Was a passing moonbeam's wile.
   An hour he sat, and read in vain,
   Nought but mirrors were his eyes;
For to and fro through his helpless brain,
  Went the dance's mysteries;
Till a gust of wind against the pane,
  Mixed with a sea-bird's cries,
And the sudden spatter of drifting rain
  Bade him mark the altered skies.
   The moon was gone, intombed in cloud;
   The wind began to rave;
The ocean heaved within its shroud,
  For the dark had built its grave;
But like ghosts brake forth, and cried aloud,
  The white crests of the wave.
   Big rain. The wind howled out, aware
   Of the tread of the watery west;
The windows shivered, back waved his hair,
  The fireside seemed the best;
But lo! a lady sat in his chair,
  With the moonlight across her breast.
   The moonbeam passed. The lady sat on.
   Her beauty was sad and white.
All but her hair with whiteness shone,
  And her hair was black as night;
And her eyes, where darkness was never gone,
  Although they were full of light.
   But her hair was wet, and wept like weeds
   On her pearly shoulders bare;
And the clear pale drops ran down like beads,
  Down her arms, to her fingers fair;
And her limbs shine through, like thin-filmed seeds,
  Her dank white robe's despair.
   She moved not, but looked in his wondering face,
   Till his blushes began to rise;
But she gazed, like one on the veiling lace,
  To something within his eyes;
A gaze that had not to do with place,
  But thought and spirit tries.

Then the voice came forth, all sweet and clear,
  Though jarred by inward pain;
She spoke like one that speaks in fear
  Of the judgment she will gain,
When the soul is full as a mountain-mere,
  And the speech, but a flowing vein.
  "Thine eyes are like mine, and thou art bold;
  Nay, heap not the dying fire;
It warms not me, I am too cold,
  Cold as the churchyard spire;
If thou cover me up with fold on fold,
  Thou kill'st not the coldness dire."
  Her voice and her beauty, like molten gold,
  Thrilled through him in burning rain.
He was on fire, and she was cold,
  Cold as the waveless main;
But his heart-well filled with woe, till it rolled
  A torrent that calmed him again.
  "Save me, Oh, save me!" she cried; and flung
  Her splendour before his feet;—
"I am weary of wandering storms among,
  And I hate the mouldy sheet;
I can dare the dark, wind-vexed and wrung,
  Not the dark where the dead things meet.
  "Ah! though a ghost, I'm a lady still—"
  The youth recoiled aghast.
With a passion of sorrow her great eyes fill;
  Not a word her white lips passed.
He caught her hand; 'twas a cold to kill,
  But he held it warm and fast.
  "What can I do to save thee, dear?"
  At the word she sprang upright.
To her ice-lips she drew his burning ear,
  And whispered—he shivered—she whispered light.
She withdrew; she gazed with an asking fear;
  He stood with a face ghost-white.
  "I wait—ah, would I might wait!" she said;
  "But the moon sinks in the tide;
Thou seest it not; I see it fade,
  Like one that may not bide.
Alas! I go out in the moonless shade;
  Ah, kind! let me stay and hide."
  He shivered, he shook, he felt like clay;
  And the fear went through his blood;
His face was an awful ashy grey,
  And his veins were channels of mud.

The lady stood in a white dismay,
  Like a half-blown frozen bud.
  "Ah, speak! am I so frightful then?
  I live; though they call it death;
I am only cold—say *dear* again"—
  But scarce could he heave a breath;
The air felt dank, like a frozen fen,
  And he a half-conscious wraith.
  "Ah, save me!" once more, with a hopeless cry,
  That entered his heart, and lay;
But sunshine and warmth and rosiness vie
  With coldness and moonlight and grey.
He spoke not. She moved not; yet to his eye,
  She stood three paces away.
  She spoke no more. Grief on her face
  Beauty had almost slain.
With a feverous vision's unseen pace
  She had flitted away again;
And stood, with a last dumb prayer for grace,
  By the window that clanged with rain.
  He stood; he stared. She had vanished quite.
  The loud wind sank to a sigh;
Grey faces without paled the face of night,
  As they swept the window by;
And each, as it passed, pressed a cheek of fright
  To the glass, with a staring eye.
  And over, afar from over the deep,
  Came a long and cadenced wail;
It rose, and it sank, and it rose on the steep
  Of the billows that build the gale.
It ceased; but on in his bosom creep
  Low echoes that tell the tale.
  He opened his lattice, and saw afar,
  Over the western sea,
Across the spears of a sparkling star,
  A moony vapour flee;
And he thought, with a pang that he could not bar,
  The lady it might be.
  He turned and looked into the room;
  And lo! it was cheerless and bare;
Empty and drear as a hopeless tomb,—
  And the lady was not there;
Yet the fire and the lamp drove out the gloom,
  As he had driven the fair.
  And up in the manhood of his breast,
  Sprang a storm of passion and shame;

It tore the pride of his fancied best
  In a thousand shreds of blame;
It threw to the ground his ancient crest,
  And puffed at his ancient name.
   He had turned a lady, and lightly clad,
  Out in the stormy cold.
Was she a ghost?—Divinely sad
  Are the guests of Hades old.
A wandering ghost? Oh! terror bad,
  That refused an earthly fold!
   And sorrow for her his shame's regret
  Into humility wept;
He knelt and he kissed the footprints wet,
  And the track by her thin robe swept;
He sat in her chair, all ice-cold yet,
  And moaned until he slept.
   He woke at dawn. The flaming sun
  Laughed at the bye-gone dark.
"I am glad," he said, "that the night is done,
  And the dream slain by the lark."
And the eye was all, until the gun
  That boomed at the sun-set—hark!
   And then, with a sudden invading blast,
  He knew that it was no dream.
And all the night belief held fast,
  Till thinned by the morning beam.
Thus radiant mornings and pale nights passed
  On the backward-flowing stream.
   He loved a lady with heaving breath,
  Red lips, and a smile alway;
And her sighs an odour inhabiteth,
  All of the rose-hued may;
But the warm bright lady was false as death,
  And the ghost is true as day.
   And the spirit-face, with its woe divine,
  Came back in the hour of sighs;
As to men who have lost their aim, and pine,
  Old faces of childhood rise:
He wept for her pleading voice, and the shine
  Of her solitary eyes.
   And now he believed in the ghost all night,
  And believed in the day as well;
And he vowed, with a sorrowing tearful might,
  All she asked, whate'er befel,
If she came to his room, in her garment white,
  Once more at the midnight knell.

She came not. He sought her in churchyards old
  That lay along the sea;
And in many a church, when the midnight tolled,
  And the moon shone wondrously;
And down to the crypts he crept, grown bold;
  But he waited in vain: ah me!
  And he pined and sighed for love so sore,
  That he looked as he were lost;
And he prayed her pardon more and more,
  As one who had sinned the most;
Till, fading at length, away he wore,
  And he was himself a ghost.
  But if he found the lady then,
  The lady sadly lost,
Or she had found 'mongst living men
  A love that was a host,
I know not, till I drop my pen,
  And am myself a ghost.

ABU MIDJAN.
      "It is only just
      To laud good wine:
      If I sit in the dust,
      So sits the vine."
  Abu Midjan sang, as he sat in chains,
For the blood of the grape was the juice of his veins.
The prophet had said, "O Faithful, drink not"—
Abu Midjan drank till his heart was hot;
Yea, he sang a song in praise of wine,
And called it good names, a joy divine.
And Saad assailed him with words of blame,
And left him in irons, a fettered flame;
But he sang of the wine as he sat in chains,
For the blood of the grape ran fast in his veins.
      "I will not think
      That the Prophet said,
      Ye shall not drink
      Of the flowing red.
      "But some weakling head,
      In its after pain,
      Moaning said,
      Drink not again.
      "But I will dare,
      With a goodly drought,
      To drink and not spare,
      Till my thirst be out.

"For as I quaff
  The liquor cool,
I do not laugh,
  Like a Christian fool;
"But my bosom fills,
  And my faith is high;
Through the emerald hills
  Goes my lightning eye.
"I see *them* hearken,
  I see them wait;
Their light eyes darken
  The diamond gate.
"I hear the float
  Of their chant divine;
Each heavenly note
  Mingles with mine.
"Can an evil thing
  Make beauty more?
Or a sinner bring
  To the heavenly door?
"'Tis the sun-rays fine
  That sink in the earth,
And are drunk by the vine,
  For its daughters' birth.
"And the liquid light,
  I drink again;
And it flows in might
  Through the shining brain,
"Making it know
  The things that are
In the earth below,
  Or the farthest star.
"I will not think
  That the Prophet said,
*Ye shall not drink
  Of the flowing Red.*
"For his promise, lo!
  Shows more divine,
When the channels o'erflow
  With the singing wine.
  "But if he did, 'tis a small annoy
  To sit in chains for a heavenly joy."
Away went the song on the light wind borne.
His head sank down, and a ripple of scorn,
At the irons that fettered his brown limbs' strength.
Waved on his lip the dark hair's length.

But sudden he lifted his head to the north—
Like a mountain-beacon his eye blazed forth:
'Twas a cloud in the distance that caught his eye,
Whence a faint clang shot on the light breeze by;
A noise and a smoke on the plain afar—
'Tis the cloud and the clang of the Moslem war.
And the light that flashed from his black eyes, lo!
Was a light that paled the red wine's glow;
And he shook his fetters in bootless ire,
And called on the Prophet, and named his sire.
But the lady of Saad heard the clang,
And she knew the far sabres his fetters rang.
Oh! she had the heart where a man might rest,
For she knew the tempest in his breast.
She rose. Ere she reached him, he called her name,
But he called not twice ere the lady came;
And he sprang to his feet, and the irons cursed,
And wild from his lips the Tecbir burst:
"Let me go," he said, "and, by Allah's fear,
At sundown I sit in my fetters here,
Or lie 'neath a heaven of starry eyes,
Kissed by moon-maidens of Paradise."
   The lady unlocked his fetters stout,
Brought her husband's horse and his armour out,
Clothed the warrior, and bid him go
An angel of vengeance upon the foe;
Then turned her in, and from the roof,
Beheld the battle, far aloof.
   Straight as an arrow she saw him go,
Abu Midjan, the singer, upon the foe.
Like home-sped lightning he pierced the cloud,
And the thunder of battle burst more loud;
And like lightning along a thunderous steep,
She saw the sickle-shaped sabres sweep,
Keen as the sunlight they dashed away
When it broke against them in flashing spray;
Till the battle ebbed o'er the plain afar,
Borne on the flow of the holy war.
As sank from the edge the sun's last flame,
Back to his bonds Abu Midjan came.
   "O lady!" he said, "'tis a mighty horse;
The Prophet himself might have rode a worse.
I felt beneath me his muscles' play,
As he tore to the battle, like fiend, away.
I forgot him, and swept at the traitor weeds,
And they fell before me like broken reeds;

Dropt their heads, as a boy doth mow
The poppies' heads with his unstrung bow.
They fled. The faithful follow at will.
I turned. And lo! he was under me still.
Give him water, lady, and barley to eat;
Then come and help me to fetter my feet."
  He went to the terrace, she went to the stall,
And tended the horse like a guest in the hall;
Then to the singer in haste returned.
The fire of the fight in his eyes yet burned;
But he said no more, as if in shame
Of the words that had burst from his lips in flame.
She left him there, as at first she found,
Seated in fetters upon the ground.
  But the sealed fountain, in pulses strong,
O'erflowed his silence, and burst in song.

      "Oh! the wine
    Of the vine
     Is a feeble thing;
    In the rattle
    Of battle
     The true grapes spring.
     "When on force
    Of the horse,
     The arm flung abroad
    Is sweeping,
    And reaping
     The harvest of God.
     "When the fear
    Of the spear
     Makes way for its blow;
    And the faithless
    Lie breathless
     The horse-hoofs below.
     "The wave-crest,
    Round the breast,
     Tosses sabres all red;
    But under,
    Its thunder
     Is dumb to the dead.
     "They drop
    From the top
     To the sear heap below;
    And deeper,
    Down steeper,
     The infidels go.

    "But bright
Is the light
  On the true-hearted breaking;
Rapturous faces,
Bent for embraces,
    Wait on his waking.
    "And he hears
In his ears
  The voice of the river,
Like a maiden,
Love-laden,
  Go wandering ever.
    "Oh! the wine
Of the vine
  May lead to the gates;
But the rattle
Of battle
  Wakes the angel who waits.
    "To the lord
Of the sword
  Open it must;
The drinker,
The thinker,
  Sits in the dust.
    "He dreams
Of the gleams
  Of their garments of white:
He misses
Their kisses,
  The maidens of light.
    "They long
For the strong,
  Who has burst through alarms,
Up, by the labour
Of stirrup and sabre,
    Up to their arms.
"Oh! the wine of the grape is a feeble ghost;
But the wine of the fight is the joy of a host."
  When Saad came home from the far pursuit,
He sat him down, and an hour was mute.
But at length he said: "Ah! wife, the fight
Had been lost full sure, but an arm of might
Sudden rose up on the crest of the war,
With its sabre that circled in rainbows afar,
Took up the battle, and drove it on—
Enoch sure, or the good St. John.

Wherever he leaped, like a lion he,
The fight was thickest, or soon to be;
Wherever he sprang, with his lion cry,
The thick of the battle soon went by.
With a headlong fear, the sinners fled;
We followed—and passed them—for they were dead.
But him who had saved us, we saw no more;
He had gone, as he came, by a secret door;
And strange to tell, in his holy force,
He wore my armour, he rode my horse."
   The lady arose, with her noble pride,
And she walked with Saad, side by side;
As she led him, a moon that would not wane,
Where Midjan counted the links of his chain!
  "I gave him thy horse, and thy armour to wear;
If I did a wrong, I am here to bear."
  "Abu Midjan, the singer of love and of wine!
The arm of the battle—it also was thine?
Rise up, shake the fetters from off thy feet;
For the lord of the battle, are fetters meet?
Drink as thou wilt—till thou be hoar—
Let Allah judge thee—I judge no more."
   Abu Midjan arose and flung aside
The clanging fetters, and thus he cried:
"If thou give me to God and his decrees,
Nor purge my sin by the shame of these;
I dare not do as I did before—
In the name of Allah, I drink no more."

AN OLD STORY.

  They were parted at last, although
    Each was tenderly dear;
As asunder their eyes did go,
    When first alone and near.
  'Tis an old story this—
    A trembling and a sigh,
A gaze in the eyes, a kiss—
    Why will it *not* go by?

A BOOK OF DREAMS.

PART I.

1.

  I lay and dreamed. The master came
    In his old woven dress;
I stood in joy, and yet in shame,
    Oppressed with earthliness.
  He stretched his arms, and gently sought
    To clasp me to his soul;

I shrunk away, because I thought
  He did not know the whole.
  I did not love him as I would,
  Embraces were not meet;
I sank before him where he stood,
  And held and kissed his feet.
    Ten years have passed away since then,
    Oft hast thou come to me;
The question scarce will rise again,
  Whether I care for thee.
    To every doubt, in thee my heart
    An answer hopes to find;
In every gladness, Lord, thou art,
  The deeper joy behind.
    And yet in other realms of life,
    Unknown temptations rise,
Unknown perplexities and strife,
  New questions and replies.
    And every lesson learnt, anew,
    The vain assurance lends
That now I know, and now can do,
  And now should see thy ends.
    So I forget I am a child,
    And act as if a man;
Who through the dark and tempest wild
  Will go, because he can.
    And so, O Lord, not yet I dare
    To clasp thee to my breast;
Though well I know that only there
  Is hid the secret rest.
    And yet I shrink not, as at first:
    Be thou the judge of guilt;
Thou knowest all my best and worst,
  Do with me as thou wilt.
    Spread thou once more thine arms abroad,
    Lay bare thy bosom's beat;
Thou shalt embrace me, O my God,
  And I will kiss thy feet.
    2.
    I stood before my childhood's home,
    Outside the belt of trees;
All round, my dreaming glances roam
  On well-known hills and leas.
    When sudden, from the westward, rushed
    A wide array of waves;

Over the subject fields they gushed
  From far-off, unknown caves.
  And up the hill they clomb and came,
  On flowing like a sea:
I saw, and watched them like a game;
  No terror woke in me.
  For just the belting trees within,
  I saw my father wait;
And should the waves the summit win,
  I would go through the gate.
  For by his side all doubt was dumb,
  And terror ceased to foam;
No great sea-billows dared to come,
  And tread the holy home.
  Two days passed by. With restless toss,
  The red flood brake its doors;
Prostrate I lay, and looked across
  To the eternal shores.
  The world was fair, and hope was nigh,
  Some men and women true;
And I was strong, and Death and I
  Would have a hard ado.
  And so I shrank. But sweet and good
  The dream came to my aid;
Within the trees my father stood,
  I must not be dismayed.
  My grief was his, not mine alone;
  The waves that burst in fears,
He heard not only with his own,
  But heard them with my ears.
  My life and death belong to thee,
  For I am thine, O God;
Thy hands have made and fashioned me,
  'Tis thine to bear the load.
  And thou shalt bear it. I will try
  To be a peaceful child,
Whom in thy arms right tenderly
  Thou carriest through the wild.
    3.
  The rich man mourns his little loss,
  And knits the brow of care;
The poor man tries to bear the cross,
  And seeks relief in prayer.
  Some gold had vanished from my purse,
  Which I had watched but ill;

I feared a lack, but feared yet worse
  Regret returning still.
   And so I knelt and prayed my prayer
   To Him who maketh strong,
That no returning thoughts of care
  Should do my spirit wrong.
   I rose in peace, in comfort went,
   And laid me down to rest;
But straight my soul grew confident
  With gladness of the blest.
   For ere the sleep that care redeems,
   My soul such visions had,
That never child in childhood's dreams
  Was more exulting glad.
   No white-robed angels floated by
   On slow, reposing wings;
I only saw, with inward eye,
  Some very common things.
   First rose the scarlet pimpernel,
   With burning purple heart;
I saw it, and I knew right well
  The lesson of its art.
   Then came the primrose, childlike flower;
   It looked me in the face;
It bore a message full of power,
  And confidence, and grace.
   And winds arose on uplands wild,
   And bathed me like a stream;
And sheep-bells babbled round the child
  Who loved them in a dream.
   Henceforth my mind was never crossed
   By thought of vanished gold,
But with it came the guardian host
  Of flowers both meek and bold.
   The loss is riches while I live,
   A joy I would not lose:
Choose ever, God, what Thou wilt give,
  Not leaving me to choose.

   "What said the flowers in whisper low,
   To soothe me into rest?"
I scarce have words—they seemed to grow
  Right out of God's own breast.
   They said, God meant the flowers He made,
   As children see the same;
They said the words the lilies said
  When Jesus looked at them.

    And if you want to hear the flowers
      Speak ancient words, all new,
    They may, if you, in darksome hours,
      Ask God to comfort you.
      4.
      Our souls, in daylight hours, awake,
      With visions sometimes teem,
    Which to the slumbering brain would take
      The form of wondrous dream.
      Thus, once, I saw a level space,
      With circling mountains nigh;
    And round it grouped all forms of grace,
      A goodly company.
      And at one end, with gentle rise,
      Stood something like a throne;
    And thither all the radiant eyes,
      As to a centre, shone.
      And on the seat the noblest form
      Of glory, dim-descried;
    His glance would quell all passion-storm,
      All doubt, and fear, and pride.
      But lo! his eyes far-fixed burn
      Adown the widening vale;
    The looks of all obedient turn,
      And soon those looks are pale.
      For, through the shining multitude,
      With feeble step and slow,
    A weary man, in garments rude,
      All falteringly did go.
      His face was white, and still-composed,
      Like one that had been dead;
    The eyes, from eyelids half unclosed,
      A faint, wan splendour shed.
      And to his brow a strange wreath clung,
      And drops of crimson hue;
    And his rough hands, oh, sadly wrung!
      Were pierced through and through.
      And not a look he turned aside;
      His eyes were forward bent;
    And slow the eyelids opened wide,
      As towards the throne he went.
      At length he reached the mighty throne,
      And sank upon his knees;
    And clasped his hands with stifled groan,
      And spake in words like these:—

"Father, I am come back—Thy will
  Is sometimes hard to do."
From all the multitude so still,
  A sound of weeping grew.
    And mournful-glad came down the One,
    And kneeled, and clasped His child;
Sank on His breast the outworn man,
  And wept until he smiled.
    And when their tears had stilled their sighs,
    And joy their tears had dried,
The people saw, with lifted eyes,
  Them seated side by side.

5.

  I lay and dreamed. Three crosses stood
  Amid the gloomy air.
Two bore two men—one was the Good;
  The third rose waiting, bare.
    A Roman soldier, coming by,
    Mistook me for the third;
I lifted up my asking eye
  For Jesus' sign or word.
    I thought He signed that I should yield,
    And give the error way.
I held my peace; no word revealed,
  No gesture uttered *nay*.
    Against the cross a scaffold stood,
    Whence easy hands could nail
The doomed upon that altar-wood,
  Whose fire burns slow and pale.
    Upon this ledge he lifted me.
    I stood all thoughtful there,
Waiting until the deadly tree
  My form for fruit should bear.
    Rose up the waves of fear and doubt,
    Rose up from heart to brain;
They shut the world of vision out,
  And thus they cried amain:
    "Ah me! my hands—the hammer's knock—
    The nails—the tearing strength!"
My soul replied: "'Tis but a shock,
  That grows to pain at length."
    "Ah me! the awful fight with death;
    The hours to hang and die;
The thirsting gasp for common breath,
  That passes heedless by!"

My soul replied: "A faintness soon
  Will shroud thee in its fold;
The hours will go,—the fearful noon
  Rise, pass—and thou art cold.
  "And for thy suffering, what to thee
  Is that? or care of thine?
Thou living branch upon the tree
  Whose root is the Divine!
  "'Tis His to care that thou endure;
  That pain shall grow or fade;
With bleeding hands hang on thy cure,
  He knows what He hath made."
  And still, for all the inward wail,
  My foot was firmly pressed;
For still the fear lest I should fail
  Was stronger than the rest.
  And thus I stood, until the strife
  The bonds of slumber brake;
I felt as I had ruined life,
  Had fled, and come awake.
  Yet I was glad, my heart confessed,
  The trial went not on;
Glad likewise I had stood the test,
  As far as it had gone.
  And yet I fear some recreant thought,
  Which now I all forget,
That painful feeling in me wrought
  Of failure, lingering yet.
  And if the dream had had its scope,
  I might have fled the field;
But yet I thank Thee for the hope,
  And think I dared not yield.
  6.
  Methinks I hear, as I lie slowly dying,
  Indulgent friends say, weeping, "*He was good.*"
I fail to speak, a faint denial trying,—
  They answer, "*His humility withstood.*"
  I, knowing better, part with love unspoken;
  And find the unknown world not all unknown.
The bonds that held me from my centre broken,
  I seek my home, the Saviour's homely throne.
  How He will greet me, I walk on and wonder;
  And think I know what I will say to Him.
I fear no sapphire floor of cloudy thunder,
  I fear no passing vision great and dim.

But He knows all my unknown weary story:
How will He judge me, pure, and good, and fair?
I come to Him in all His conquered glory,
 Won from such life as I went dreaming there!
 I come; I fall before Him, faintly saying:
"Ah, Lord, shall I thy loving favour win?
Earth's beauties tempted me; my walk was straying—
 I have no honour—but may I come in?"
 "I know thee well. Strong prayer did keep me stable;
 To me the earth is very lovely too.
Thou shouldst have come to me to make thee able
 To love it greatly—but thou hast got through."

A BOOK OF DREAMS.
PART II.
1.
Lord of the world's undying youth,
What joys are in thy might!
What beauties of the inner truth,
And of the outer sight!
And when the heart is dim and sad,
Too weak for wisdom's beam,
Thou sometimes makest it right glad
With but a childish dream.
* * * * *

Lo! I will dream this windy day;
 No sunny spot is bare;
Dull vapours, in uncomely play,
 Are weltering through the air.
If I throw wide my windowed breast
 To all the blasts that blow,
My soul will rival in unrest
 Those tree-tops—how they go!
 But I will dream like any child;
 For, lo! a mighty swan,
With radiant plumage undented,
 And folded airy van,
With serpent neck all proudly bent,
 And stroke of swarthy oar,
Dreams on to me, by sea-maids sent
 Over the billows hoar.
 For in a wave-worn rock I lie;
 Outside, the waters foam;
And echoes of old storms go by
 Within my sea-built dome.
The waters, half the gloomy way,
 Beneath its arches come;

Throbbing to unseen billows' play,
  The green gulfs waver dumb.
A dawning twilight through the cave
  In moony gleams doth go,
Half from the swan above the wave,
  Half from the swan below.
Close to my feet she gently drifts,
  Among the glistening things;
She stoops her crowny head, and lifts
  White shoulders of her wings.
  Oh! earth is rich with many a nest,
  Deep, soft, and ever new,
Pure, delicate, and full of rest;
  But dearest there are two.
I would not tell them but to minds
  That are as white as they;
If others hear, of other kinds,
  I wish them far away.
  Upon the neck, between the wings,
  Of a white, sailing swan,
A flaky bed of shelterings—
  There you will find the one.
The other—well, it will not out,
  Nor need I tell it you;
I've told you one, and need you doubt,
  When there are only two?
  Fulfil old dreams, O splendid bird,
  Me o'er the waters bear;
Sure never ocean's face was stirred
  By any ship so fair!
Sure never whiteness found a dress,
  Upon the earth to go,
So true, profound, and rich, unless
  It was the falling snow.
  With quick short flutter of each wing
  Half-spread, and stooping crown,
She calls me; and with one glad spring
  I nestle in the down.
Plunges the bark, then bounds aloft,
  With lessening dip and rise.
Round curves her neck with motion soft—
  Sure those are woman's eyes.
  One stroke unseen, with oary feet,
  One stroke—away she sweeps;
Over the waters pale we fleet,
  Suspended in the deeps.

And round the sheltering rock, and lo!
  The tumbling, weltering sea!
On to the west, away we go,
  Over the waters free!
    Her motions moulded to the wave,
    Her billowy neck thrown back,
With slow strong pulse, stately and grave,
    She cleaves a rippling track.
And up the mounting wave we glide,
    With climbing sweeping blow;
And down the steep, far-sloping side,
    To flowing vales below.
    I hear the murmur of the deep
    In countless ripples pass,
Like talking children in their sleep,
    Like winds in reedy grass.
And through some ruffled feathers, I
    The glassy rolling mark,
With which the waves eternally
    Roll on from dawn to dark.
    The night is blue, the stars aglow;
    In solemn peace o'erhead
The archless depth of heaven; below,
    The murmuring, heaving bed.
A thickened night, it heaveth on,
    A fallen earthly sky;
The shadows of its stars alone
    Are left to know it by.
    What faints across the lifted loop
    Of cloud-veil upward cast?
With sea-veiled limbs, a sleeping group
    Of Nereids dreaming past.
Swim on, my boat; who knows but I,
    Ere night sinks to her grave,
May see in splendour pale float by
    The Venus of the wave?
    2.
    In the night, round a lady dreaming—
    A queen among the dreams—
Came the silent sunset streaming,
    Mixed with the voice of streams.
A silver fountain springing
    Blossoms in molten gold;
And the airs of the birds float ringing
    Through harmonies manifold.

She lies in a watered valley;
  Her garden melts away
Through foot-path and curving alley
  Into the wild wood grey.
And the green of the vale goes creeping
  To the feet of the rugged hills,
Where the moveless rocks are keeping
  The homes of the wandering rills.
  And the hues of the flowers grow deeper,
    Till they dye her very brain;
And their scents, like the soul of a sleeper,
  Wander and waver and rain.
For dreams have a wealth of glory
  That daylight cannot give:
Ah God! make the hope a story—
  Bid the dreams arise and live.
  She lay and gazed at the flowers,
    Till her soul's own garden smiled
With blossom-o'ershaded bowers,
  Great colours and splendours wild.
And her heart filled up with gladness,
  Till it could only ache;
And it turned aside to sadness,
  As if for pity's sake.
  And a fog came o'er the meadows,
    And the rich hues fainting lay;
Came from the woods the shadows,
  Came from the rocks the grey.
And the sunset thither had vanished,
  Where the sunsets always go;
And the sounds of the stream were banished,
  As if slain by frost and snow.
  And the flowers paled fast and faster,
    And they crumbled fold on fold,
Till they looked like the stained plaster
  Of a cornice in ruin old.
And they blackened and shrunk together,
  As if scorched by the breath of flame,
With a sad perplexity whether
  They were or were not the same.
  And she saw herself still lying,
    And smiling on, the while;
And the smile, instead of dying,
  Was fixed in an idiot smile.
And the lady arose in sorrow
  Out of her sleep's dark stream;

But her dream made dark the morrow,
  And she told me the haunting dream.
  Alas! dear lady, I know it,
  The dream that all is a dream;
The joy with the doubt below it
  That the bright things only seem.
One moment of sad commotion,
  And one of doubt's withering rule—
And the great wave-pulsing ocean
  Is only a gathered pool.
  And the flowers are spots of painting,
  Of lifeless staring hue;
Though your heart is sick to fainting,
  They say not a word to you.
And the birds know nought of gladness,
  They are only song-machines;
And a man is a skilful madness,
  And the women pictured queens.
  And fiercely we dig the fountain,
  To know the water true;
And we climb the crest of the mountain,
  To part it from the blue.
But we look too far before us
  For that which is more than nigh;
Though the sky is lofty o'er us,
  We are always in the sky.
  And the fog, o'er the roses that creepeth,
  Steams from the unknown sea,
In the dark of the soul that sleepeth,
  And sigheth constantly,
Because o'er the face of its waters
  The breathing hath not gone;
And instead of glad sons and daughters,
  Wild things are moaning on.
  When the heart knows well the Father,
  The eyes will be always day;
But now they grow dim the rather
  That the light is more than they.
Believe, amidst thy sorrows,
  That the blight that swathes the earth
Is only a shade that borrows
  Life from thy spirit's dearth.
  God's heart is the fount of beauty;
  Thy heart is its visible well;
If it vanish, do thou thy duty,
  That necromantic spell;

And thy heart to the Father crying
  Will fill with waters deep;
Thine eyes may say, *Beauty is dying;*
  But thy spirit, *She goes to sleep.*
    And I fear not, thy fair soul ever
    Will smile as thy image smiled;
It had fled with a sudden shiver,
  And thy body lay beguiled.
Let the flowers and thy beauty perish;
  Let them go to the ancient dust.
But the hopes that the children cherish,
  They are the Father's trust.

3.

  A great church in an empty square,
    A place of echoing tones;
Feet pass not oft enough to wear
  The grass between the stones.
    The jarring sounds that haunt its gates,
    Like distant thunders boom;
The boding heart half-listening waits,
  As for a coming doom.
    The door stands wide, the church is bare,
    Oh, horror, ghastly, sore!
A gulf of death, with hideous stare,
  Yawns in the earthen floor;
    As if the ground had sunk away
    Into a void below:
Its shapeless sides of dark-hued clay
  Hang ready aye to go.
    I am myself a horrid grave,
    My very heart turns grey;
This charnel-hole,—will no one save
  And force my feet away?
    The changing dead are there, I know,
    In terror ever new;
Yet down the frightful slope I go,
  That downward goeth too.
    Beneath the caverned floor I hie,
    And seem, with anguish dull,
To enter by the empty eye
  Into a monstrous skull.
    Stumbling on what I dare not guess,
    And wading through the gloom,
Less deep the shades my eyes oppress,
  I see the awful tomb.

My steps have led me to a door,
  With iron clenched and barred;
Grim Death hides there a ghastlier store,
  Great spider in his ward.
    The portals shake, the bars are bowed,
    As if an earthy wind
That never bore a leaf or cloud
  Were pressing hard behind.
    They shake, they groan, they outward strain.
    What sight, of dire dismay
Will freeze its form upon my brain,
  And turn it into clay?
    They shake, they groan, they bend, they crack;
    The bars, the doors divide:
A flood of glory at their back
  Hath burst the portals wide.
  Flows in the light of vanished days,
  The joy of long-set moons;
The flood of radiance billowy plays,
  In sweet-conflicting tunes.
    The gulf is filled with flashing tides,
    An awful gulf no more;
A maze of ferns clothes all its sides,
  Of mosses all its floor.
    And, floating through the streams, appear
    Such forms of beauty rare,
As every aim at beauty here
  Had found its *would be* there.
    I said: 'Tis well no hand came nigh,
    To turn my steps astray;
'Tis good we cannot choose but die,
  That life may have its way.
    4.
    Before I sleep, some dreams draw nigh,
    Which are not fancy mere;
For sudden lights an inward eye,
  And wondrous things appear.
    Thus, unawares, with vision wide,
    A steep hill once I saw,
In faint dream lights, which ever hide
  Their fountain and their law.
    And up and down the hill reclined
    A host of statues old;
Such wondrous forms as you might find
  Deep under ancient mould.

They lay, wild scattered, all along,
  And maimed as if in fight;
But every one of all the throng
  Was precious to the sight.
    Betwixt the night and hill they ranged,
    In dead composure cast.
As suddenly the dream was changed,
  And all the wonder past.
    The hill remained; but what it bore
    Was broken reedy stalks,
Bent hither, thither, drooping o'er,
  Like flowers o'er weedy walks.
    For each dim form of marble rare,
    Bent a wind-broken reed;
So hangs on autumn-field, long-bare,
  Some tall and straggling weed.
    The autumn night hung like a pall,
    Hung mournfully and dead;
And if a wind had waked at all,
  It had but moaned and fled.
    5.
    I lay and dreamed. Of thought and sleep
    Was born a heavenly joy:
I dreamed of two who always keep
  Me happy as a boy.
    I was with them. My heart-bells rung
    With joy my heart above;
Their present heaven my earth o'erhung,
  And earth was glad with love.
    The dream grew troubled. Crowds went on,
    And sought their varied ends;
Till stream on stream, the crowds had gone,
  And swept away my friends.
    I was alone. A miry road
    I followed, all in vain;
No well-known hill the landscape showed,
  It was a wretched plain;
    Where mounds of rubbish, ugly pits,
    And brick-fields scarred the globe;
Those wastes where desolation sits
  Without her ancient robe.
    A drizzling rain proclaimed the skies
    As wretched as the earth;
I wandered on, and weary sighs
  Were all my lot was worth.

When sudden, as I turned my way,
  Burst in the ocean-waves:
And lo! a blue wild-dancing bay
  Fantastic rocks and caves!
  I wept with joy. Ah! sometimes so,
  In common daylight grief,
A beauty to the heart will go,
  And bring the heart relief.
  And, wandering, reft of hope or friend,
  If such a thing should be,
One day we take the downward bend,
  And lo, Eternity!
  I wept with joy, delicious tears,
  Which dreams alone bestow;
Until, mayhap, from out the years
  We sleep, and further go.
  6.
  Now I will mould a dream, awake,
  Which I, asleep, would dream;
From all the forms of fancy take
  One that shall also seem;
Seem in my verse (if not my brain),
  Which sometimes may rejoice
In airy forms of Fancy's train,
  Though nobler are my choice.
  Some truth o'er all the land may lie
  In children's dreams at night;
They do not build the charmed sky
  That domes them with delight.
And o'er the years that follow soon,
  So all unlike the dreams,
Wander their odours, gleams their moon,
  And flow their winds and streams.
  Now I would dream that I awake
  In scent of cool night air,
Above me star-clouds close and break;
  Beneath—where am I, where?
A strange delight pervades my breast,
  Of ancient pictures dim,
Where fair forms on the waters rest,
  Or in the breezes swim.
  I rest on arms as soft as strong,
  Great arms of woman-mould;
My head is pillowed whence a song,
  In many a rippling fold,
O'erfloods me from its bubbling spring:

A Titan goddess bears
Me, floating on her unseen wing,
  Through gracious midnight airs.
  And I am borne o'er sleeping seas,
  O'er murmuring ears of corn,
Over the billowy tops of trees,
  O'er roses pale till morn.
Over the lake—ah! nearer float,
  Down on the water's breast;
Let me look deep, and gazing doat
  On that white lily's nest.
  The harebell's bed, as o'er we pass,
  Swings all its bells about;
From waving blades of polished grass,
  Flash moony splendours out.
Old homes we brush in wooded glades;
  No eyes at windows shine;
For all true men and noble maids
  Are out in dreams like mine.
  And foam-bell-kisses drift and break
  From wind-waves of the South
Against my brow and eyes awake,
  And yet I see no mouth.
Light laughter ripples down the air,
  Light sighs float up below;
And o'er me ever, radiant pair,
  The Queen's great star-eyes go.
  And motion like a dreaming wave
  Wafts me in gladness dim
Through air just cool enough to lave
  With sense each conscious limb.
But ah! the dream eludes the rhyme,
  As dreams break free from sleep;
The dream will keep its own free time,
  In mazy float or sweep.
  And thought too keen for joy awakes,
  As on the horizon far,
A dead pale light the circle breaks,
  But not a dawning star.
No, there I cannot, dare not go;
  Pale women wander there;
With cold fire murderous eyeballs glow;
  And children see despair.
  The joy has lost its dreamy zest;
  I feel a pang of loss;
My wandering hand o'er mounds of rest

Finds only mounds of moss.
Beneath the bare night-stars I lie;
  Cold winds are moaning past:
Alas! the earth with grief will die,
  The great earth is aghast.
  I look above—there dawns no face;
  Around—no footsteps come;
No voice inhabits this great space;
  God knows, but keepeth dumb.
I wake, and know that God is by,
  And more than dreams will give;
And that the hearts that moan and die,
  Shall yet awake and live.

TO AURELIO SAFFI.

To God and man be simply true:
Do as thou hast been wont to do:
Or, Of the old more in the new:
Mean all the same when said to you.
  I love thee. Thou art calm and strong;
Firm in the right, mild to the wrong;
Thy heart, in every raging throng,
A chamber shut for prayer and song.
  Defeat thou know'st not, canst not know;
Only thy aims so lofty go,
They need as long to root and grow
As any mountain swathed in snow.
  Go on and prosper, holy friend.
I, weak and ignorant, would lend
A voice, thee, strong and wise, to send
Prospering onward, without end.

SONNET.

To A.M.D.
  Methinks I see thee, lying calm and low,
    Silent and dark within thy earthy bed;
    Thy mighty hands, in which I trusted, dead,
Resting, with thy long arms, from work or blow;
And the night-robe, around thy tall form, flow
  Down from the kingly face, and from the head,
  Save by its thick dark curls, uncovered—
My brother, dear from childhood, lying so!
Not often since thou went'st, I think of thee,
  (With inward cares and questionings oppressed);
  And yet, ere long, I seek thee in thy rest,
And bring thee home my heart, as full, as free,
As sure that thou wilt take me tenderly,
  As then when youth and nature made us blest.

A MEMORIAL OF AFRICA.
I.
Upon a rock, high on a mountain side,
Thousands of feet above the lake-sea's lip,
A rock in which old waters' rise and dip,
Plunge and recoil, and backward eddying tide
Had, age-long, worn, while races lived and died,
  Involved channels, where the sea-weed's drip
  Followed the ebb; and now earth-grasses sip
Fresh dews from heaven, whereby on earth they bide—
  I sat and gazed southwards. A dry flow
Of withering wind blew on my drooping strength
From o'er the awful desert's burning length.
  Behind me piled, away and upward go
Great sweeps of savage mountains—up, away,
Where panthers roam, and snow gleams all the day.
II.
Ah, God! the world needs many hours to make;
  Nor hast thou ceased the making of it yet,
  But wilt be working on when Death hath set
A new mound in some churchyard for my sake.
On flow the centuries without a break.
  Uprise the mountains, ages without let.
  The mosses suck the rock's breast, rarely wet.
Years more than past, the young earth yet will take.
  But in the dumbness of the rolling time,
No veil of silence will encompass me—
Thou wilt not once forget, and let me be:
  I easier think that thou, as I my rhyme,
Wouldst rise, and with a tenderness sublime
Unfold a world, that I, thy child, might see.

A GIFT.
  My gift would find thee fast asleep,
    And arise a dream in thee;
  A violet sky o'er the roll and sweep
    Of a purple and pallid sea;
And a crescent moon from my sky should creep
    In the golden dream to thee.
    Thou shouldst lay thee down, and sadly list
    To the wail of our cold birth-time;
And build thee a temple, glory-kissed,
    In the heart of the sunny clime;
Its columns should rise in a music-mist,
    And its roofs in a spirit-rhyme.
    Its pillars the solemn hills should bind
    'Neath arches of starry deeps;

Its floor the earth all veined and lined;
  Its organ the ocean-sweeps;
And, swung in the hands of the grey-robed wind,
  Its censers the blossom-heaps.
   And 'tis almost done; for in this my rhyme,
  Thanks to thy mirror-soul,
Thou wilt see the mountains, and hear the chime
  Of the waters after the roll;
And the stars of my sky thy sky will climb,
  And with heaven roof in the whole.

THE MAN OF SONGS.

  "Thou wanderest in the land of dreams,
    O man of many songs;
To thee the actual only seems—
    No realm to thee belongs."
  "Seest thou those mountains in the east,
    O man of ready aim?"
"'T is only vapours that thou seest,
    In mountain form and name."
  "Nay, nay, I know them all too well,
    Each ridge, and peak, and dome;
In that cloud-land, in one high dell,
    Nesteth my little home."

BETTER THINGS.

  Better to smell a violet,
Than sip the careless wine;
Better to list one music tone,
Than watch the jewels' shine.
  Better to have the love of one,
Than smiles like morning dew;
Better to have a living seed
Than flowers of every hue.
  Better to feel a love within,
Than be lovely to the sight;
Better a homely tenderness
Than beauty's wild delight.
  Better to love than be beloved,
Though lonely all the day;
Better the fountain in the heart,
Than the fountain by the way.
  Better a feeble love to God,
Than for woman's love to pine;
Better to have the making God
Than the woman made divine.
  Better be fed by mother's hand,
Than eat alone at will;

Better to trust in God, than say:
My goods my storehouse fill.
　Better to be a little wise
Than learned overmuch;
Better than high are lowly thoughts,
For truthful thoughts are such.
　Better than thrill a listening crowd,
Sit at a wise man's feet;
But better teach a child, than toil
To make thyself complete.
　Better to walk the realm unseen,
Than watch the hour's event;
Better the smile of God alway,
Than the voice of men's consent.
　Better to have a quiet grief
Than a tumultuous joy;
Better than manhood, age's face,
If the heart be of a boy.
　Better the thanks of one dear heart,
Than a nation's voice of praise;
Better the twilight ere the dawn,
Than yesterday's mid-blaze.
　Better a death when work is done,
Than earth's most favoured birth;
Better a child in God's great house
Than the king of all the earth.

THE JOURNEY.

Hark, the rain is on my roof!
Every sound drops through the dark
On my soul with dull reproof,
Like a half-extinguished spark.
I! alas, how am I here,
In the midnight and alone?
Caught within a net of fear!
All my dreams of beauty gone!
　I will rise: I must go forth.
Better face the hideous night,
Better dare the unseen north,
Than be still without the light!
Black wind rushing round my brow,
Sown with stinging points of rain!
Place or time I know not now—
I am here, and so is pain!
　I will leave the sleeping street,
Hie me forth on darker roads.
Ah! I cannot stay my feet,

Onward, onward, something goads.
I will take the mountain path,
Beard the storm within its den,
Know the worst of this dim wrath,
Vexing thus the souls of men.
   Chasm 'neath chasm! rock piled on rock:
Roots, and crumbling earth, and stones!
Hark, the torrent's thundering shock!
Hark, the swaying pine tree's groans!
Ah, I faint, I fall, I die!
Sink to nothingness away!—
Lo, a streak upon the sky!
Lo, the opening eye of day!
   II.
Mountain heights that lift their snows
O'er a valley green and low;
And a winding path, that goes
Guided by the river's flow;
And a music rising ever,
As of peace and low content,
From the pebble-paven river
As an odour upward sent.
   And a sighing of the storm
Far away amid the hills,
Like the humming of a swarm
That the summer forest fills;
And a frequent fall of rain
From a cloud with ragged weft;
And a burst of wind amain
From the mountain's sudden cleft.
   Then a night that hath a moon,
Staining all the cloudy white;
Sinking with a soundless tune
Deep into the spirit's night.
Then a morning clear and soft,
Amber on the purple hills;
Warm high day of summer, oft
Cooled by wandering windy rills.
   Joy to travel thus along,
With the universe around!
I the centre of the throng;
Every sight and every sound
Speeding with its burden laden,
Speeding homewards to my soul!
Mine the eye the stars are made in!
I the heart of all this whole!

III.
Hills retreat on either hand,
Sinking down into the plain;
Slowly through the level land
Glides the river to the main.
What is that before me, white,
Gleaming through the dusky air?
Dimmer in the gathering night;
Still beheld, I know not where?
  Is it but a chalky ridge,
Bared by many a trodden mark?
Or a river-spanning bridge,
Miles away into the dark?
Or the foremost leaping waves
Of the everlasting sea,
Where the Undivided laves
Time with its eternity?
  No, tis but an eye-made sight,
In my brain a fancied gleam;
Or a thousand things as white,
Set in darkness, well might seem.
There it wavers, shines, is gone;
What it is I cannot tell;
When the morning star hath shone,
I shall see and know it well.
  Onward, onward through the night!
Matters it I cannot see?
I am moving in a might,
Dwelling in the dark and me.
Up or down, or here or there,
I can never be alone;
My own being tells me where
God is as the Father known.

IV.
  Joy! O joy! the Eastern sea
Answers to the Eastern sky;
Wide and featured gloriously
With swift billows bursting high.
Nearer, nearer, oh! the sheen
On a thousand waves at once!
Oh! the changing crowding green!
Oh my beating heart's response!
  Down rejoicing to the strand,
Where the sea-waves shore-ward lean,
Curve their graceful heads, and stand
Gleaming with ethereal green,

Then in foam fall heavily—
This is what I saw at night!
Lo, a boat! I'll forth on thee,
Dancing-floor for my delight.
  From the bay, wind-winged, we glance;
Sea-winds seize me by the hair!
What a terrible expanse!
How the ocean tumbles there!
I am helpless here afloat,
For the wild waves know not me;
Gladly would I change my boat
For the snow wings of the sea!
  Look below. Each watery whirl
Cast in beauty's living mould!
Look above! Each feathery curl
Faintly tinged with morning gold!—
Oh, I tremble with the gush
Of an everlasting youth!
Love and fear together rush:
I am free in God, the Truth!
  PRAYER.
  We doubt the word that tells us: Ask,
  And ye shall have your prayer;
We turn our thoughts as to a task,
  With will constrained and rare.
  And yet we have; these scanty prayers
  Yield gold without alloy:
O God! but he that trusts and dares
  Must have a boundless joy.
  REST.
  When round the earth the Father's hands
  Have gently drawn the dark;
Sent off the sun to fresher lands,
  And curtained in the lark;
'Tis sweet, all tired with glowing day,
  To fade with faded light;
To lie once more, the old weary way,
  Upfolded in the night.
  A mother o'er the couch may bend,
  And rose-leaf kisses heap:
In soothing dreams with sleep they blend,
  Till even in dreams we sleep.
And, if we wake while night is dumb,
  'Tis sweet to turn and say,
It is an hour ere dawning come,
  And I will sleep till day.

II.
There is a dearer, warmer bed,
  Where one all day may lie,
Earth's bosom pillowing the head,
  And let the world go by.
Instead of mother's love-lit eyes,
  The church's storied pane,
All blank beneath cold starry skies,
  Or sounding in the rain.
    The great world, shouting, forward fares:
  This chamber, hid from none,
Hides safe from all, for no one cares
  For those whose work is done.
Cheer thee, my heart, though tired and slow
  An unknown grassy place
Somewhere on earth is waiting now
  To rest thee from thy race.

III.
There is a calmer than all calms,
  A quiet more deep than death:
A folding in the Father's palms,
  A breathing in his breath;
A rest made deeper by alarms
  And stormy sounds combined:
The child within its mother's arms
  Sleeps sounder for the wind.
    There needs no curtained bed to hide
  The world with all its wars,
Nor grassy cover to divide
  From sun and moon and stars
A window open to the skies,
  A sense of changeless life,
With oft returning still surprise
  Repels the sounds of strife.

IV.
As one bestrides a wild scared horse
  Beneath a stormy moon,
And still his heart, with quiet force,
  Beats on its own calm tune;
So if my heart with trouble now
  Be throbbing in my breast,
Thou art my deeper heart, and Thou,
  O God, dost ever rest.
    When mighty sea-winds madly blow,
  And tear the scattered waves;
As still as summer woods, below

  Lie darkling ocean caves:
The wind of words may toss my heart,
  But what is that to me!
'Tis but a surface storm—Thou art
  My deep, still, resting sea.
  TO A.J. SCOTT.
  WITH THE FOLLOWING POEM.
  I walked all night: the darkness did not yield.
Around me fell a mist, a weary rain,
Enduring long; till a faint dawn revealed
  A temple's front, cloud-curtained on the plain.
Closed were the lofty doors that led within;
But by a wicket one might entrance gain.
  O light, and awe, and silence! Entering in,
The blackness and chaotic rain were lost
In hopeful spaces. Then I heard a thin
  Sweet sound of voices low, together tossed,
As if they sought a harmony to find
Which they knew once; but none of all that host
  Could call the far-fled music back to mind.
Loud voices, distance-low, wandered along
The pillared paths, and up the arches twined
  With sister-arches, rising, throng on throng,
Up to the roof's dim distance. If sometimes
Self-gathered voices made a burst of song,
  Straightway I heard again but as the chimes
Of many bells through Sabbath morning sent,
Each its own tale to tell of heavenly climes.
  Yet such the hope, one might be well content
Here to be low, and lowly keep a door;
For like Truth's herald, solemnly that went,
  I heard thy voice, and humbly loved it more,
Walking the word-sea to this ear of mine,
Than any voice of power I heard before.
  Yet as the harp may, tremulous, combine
Low ghostlike sounds with organ's loudest tone,
Let not my music fear to come to thine:
  Thy heart, with organ-tempests of its own,
Will hear Aeolian sighs from thin chords blown.
  LIGHT.
  First-born of the creating Voice!
Minister of God's spirit, who wast sent
To wait upon Him first, what time He went
Moving about 'mid the tumultuous noise
Of each unpiloted element
Upon the face of the void formless deep!

Thou who didst come unbodied and alone,
Ere yet the sun was set his rule to keep,
Or ever the moon shone,
Or e'er the wandering star-flocks forth were driven!
Thou garment of the Invisible, whose skirt
Falleth on all things from the lofty heaven!
Thou Comforter, be with me as thou wert
When first I longed for words, to be
A radiant garment for my thought, like thee.
   We lay us down in sorrow,
Wrapt in the old mantle of our mother Night;
In vexing dreams we 'strive until the morrow;
Grief lifts our eyelids up—and lo, the light!
The sunlight on the wall! And visions rise
Of shining leaves that make sweet melodies;
Of wind-borne waves with thee upon their crests;
Of rippled sands on which thou rainest down;
Of quiet lakes that smooth for thee their breasts;
Of clouds that show thy glory as their own.
O joy! O joy! the visions are gone by,
Light, gladness, motion, are Reality!
   Thou art the god of earth. The skylark springs
Far up to catch thy glory on his wings;
And thou dost bless him first that highest soars.
The bee comes forth to see thee; and the flowers
Worship thee all day long, and through the skies
Follow thy journey with their earnest eyes.
River of life, thou pourest on the woods;
And on thy waves float forth the wakening buds;
The trees lean towards thee, and, in loving pain,
Keep turning still to see thee yet again.
And nothing in thine eyes is mean or low:
Where'er thou art, on every side,
All things are glorified;
And where thou canst not come, there thou dost throw
Beautiful shadows, made out of the Dark,
That else were shapeless. Loving thou dost mark
The sadness on men's faces, and dost seek
To make all things around of hope and gladness speak.
   And men have worshipped thee.
The Persian, on his mountain-top,
Kneeling doth wait until thy sun go up,
God-like in his serenity.
All-giving, and none-gifted, he draws near;
And the wide earth waits till his face appear—
Longs patient. And the herald glory leaps

Along the ridges of the outlying clouds,
Climbing the heights of all their towering steeps;
And a quiet multitudinous laughter crowds
The universal face, as, silently,
Up cometh he, the never-closing eye.
Symbol of Deity! men could not be
Farthest from truth when they were kneeling unto thee.
   Thou plaything of the child,
When from the water's surface thou dost fall
In mazy dance, ethereal motion wild,
Like his own thoughts, upon the chamber wall;
Or through the dust darting in long thin streams!
How I have played with thee, and longed to climb
On sloping ladders of thy moted beams!
And how I loved thee falling from the moon!
And most about the mellow harvest-time,
When night had softly settled down,
And thou from her didst flow, a sea of love.
And then the stars, ah me! that flashed above
And the ghost-stars that shimmered in the tide!
While here and there mysterious earthly shining
Came forth of windows from the hill and glen;
Each ray of thine so wondrously entwining
With household love and rest of weary men.
And still I am a child, thank God! To see
Thee streaming from a bit of broken glass,
That else on the brown earth lay undescried,
Is a high joy, a glorious thing to me,
A spark that lights the light of joy within,
A thought of Hope to Prophecy akin,
That from my spirit fruitless will not pass.
   Thou art the joy of Age:
The sun is dear even when long shadows fall.
Forth to the sunlight the old man doth crawl,
Enlivened like the bird in his poor cage.
Close by the door, no further, in his chair
The old man sits; and sitteth there
His soul within him, like a child that lies
Half dreaming, with his half-shut eyes,
At close of a long afternoon in summer;
High ruins round him, ancient ruins, where
The raven is almost the only comer;
And there he broods in wonderment
On the celestial glory sent
Through the rough loopholes, on the golden bloom
That waves above the cornice on the wall,

Where lately dwelt the echoes of the room;
And drinking in the yellow lights that lie
Upon the ivy tapestry.
So dreams the old man's soul, that is not old,
But sleepy 'mid the ruins that infold.
   What meanings various thou callest forth
Upon the face of the still passive earth!
Even like a lord of music bent
Over his instrument;
Whether, at hour of sovereign noon,
Infinite cataracts sheet silent down;
Or a strange yellow radiance slanting pass
Betwixt long shadows o'er the meadow grass,
When from the lower edge of a dark cloud
The sun at eve his blessing head hath bowed;
Whether the moon lift up her shining shield,
High on the peak of a cloud-hill revealed;
Or crescent, low, wandering sun-dazed away,
Unconscious of her own star-mingled ray,
Her still face seeming more to think than see,
She makes the pale world lie in dreams of thee.
Each hour of day, each hour of thoughtful night,
Hath a new poem in the changing light.
   Of highest unity the sole emblem!
In whom all colours that our eyes can see
In rainbow, moonbow, or in opal gem,
Unite in living oneness, purity,
And operative power! whose every part
Is beauty to the eyes, and truth unto the heart!
Outspread in yellow sands, blue sea and air,
Green growing corn, and scarlet poppies there;—
Regent of colours, thou, the undefiled!
Whether in dark eyes of the laughing child,
Or in the vast white cloud that floats away,
Bearing upon its breast a brown moon-ray;
The universal painter, who dost fling
Thy overflowing skill on everything!
The thousand hues and shades upon the flowers,
Are all the pastime of thy leisure hours;
And all the gems and ores that hidden be,
Are dead till they are looked upon by thee.
    Everywhere,
Thou art shining through the air;
Every atom from another
Takes thee, gives thee to his brother;
Continually,

Thou art falling on the sea,
Bathing the deep woods down below,
Making the sea-flowers bud and blow;
Silently,
Thou art working ardently,
Bringing from the night of nought
Into being and to thought;
Influences
Every beam of thine dispenses,
Powerful, varied, reaching far,
Differing in every star.
Not an iron rod can lie
In circle of thy beamy eye,
But thy look doth change it so
That it cannot choose but show
Thou, the worker, hast been there;
Yea, sometimes, on substance rare,
Thou dost leave thy ghostly mark
In what men do call the dark.
Doer, shower, mighty teacher!
Truth-in-beauty's silent preacher!
Universal something sent
To shadow forth the Excellent!
   When the firstborn affections,
Those winged seekers of the world within,
That search about in all directions,
Some bright thing for themselves to win,
Through unmarked forest-paths, and gathering fogs,
And stony plains, and treacherous bogs,
Long, long, have followed faces fair,
Fair faces without souls, that vanished into air;
And darkness is around them and above,
Desolate, with nought to love;
And through the gloom on every side,
Strange dismal forms are dim descried;
And the air is as the breath
From the lips of void-eyed Death;
And the knees are bowed in prayer
To the Stronger than Despair;
Then the ever-lifted cry,
Give us light, or we shall die,
Cometh to the Father's ears,
And He listens, and He hears:
And when men lift up their eyes,
Lo, Truth slow dawning in the skies!
'Tis as if the sun gleamed forth

Through the storm-clouds of the north.
And when men would name this Truth,
Giver of gladness and of youth,
They can call it nought but Light—
'Tis the morning, 'twas the night.
Yea, every thought of hope outspread
On the mountain's misty head,
Is a fresh aurora, sent
Through the spirit's firmament,
Telling, through the vapours dun,
Of the coming, coming sun.
   All things most excellent
Are likened unto thee, excellent thing!
Yea, He who from the Father forth was sent,
Came the true Light, light to our hearts to bring;
The Word of God, the telling of His thought;
The Light of God, the making-visible;
The far-transcending glory brought
In human form with man to dwell;
The dazzling gone; the power not less
To show, irradiate, and bless;
The gathering of the primal rays divine,
Informing chaos, to a pure sunshine!
   Death, darkness, nothingness!
Life, light, and blessedness!
   * * * * *
   Dull horrid pools no motion making;
No bubble on the surface breaking;
Through the dead heavy air, no sound;
Asleep and moveless on the marshy ground.
   * * * * *
   Rushing winds and snow-like drift,
Forceful, formless, fierce, and swift;
Hair-like vapours madly riven;
Waters smitten into dust;
Lightning through the turmoil driven,
Aimless, useless, yet it must.
   * * * * *
   Gentle winds through forests calling;
Big waves on the sea-shore falling;
Bright birds through the thick leaves glancing;
Light boats on the big waves dancing;
Children in the clear pool laving;
Mountain streams glad music giving;
Yellow corn and green grass waving;
Long-haired, bright-eyed maidens living;

Light on all things, even as now—
God, our Father, it is Thou!
Light, O Radiant! thou didst come abroad,
To mediate 'twixt our ignorance and God;
Forming ever without form;
Showing, but thyself unseen;
Pouring stillness on the storm;
Making life where death had been!
If thou, Light, didst cease to be,
Death and Chaos soon were out,
Weltering o'er the slimy sea,
Riding on the whirlwind's rout;
And if God did cease to be,
O Beloved! where were we?

   Father of Lights, pure and unspeakable,
On whom no changing shadow ever fell!
Thy light we know not, are content to see;
And shall we doubt because we know not Thee?
Or, when thy wisdom cannot be expressed,
Fear lest dark vapours dwell within thy breast?
Nay, nay, ye shadows on our souls descending!
Ye bear good witness to the light on high,
Sad shades of something 'twixt us and the sky!
And this word, known and unknown radiant blending,
Shall make us rest, like children in the night,—
Word infinite in meaning: *God is Light.*
We walk in mystery all the shining day
Of light unfathomed that bestows our seeing,
Unknown its source, unknown its ebb and flow:
Thy living light's eternal fountain-play
In ceaseless rainbow pulse bestows our being—
Its motions, whence or whither, who shall know?
O Light, if I had said all I could say
Of thy essential glory and thy might,
Something within my heart unsaid yet lay,
And there for lack of words unsaid must stay:
For *God is Light.*

  TO A.J. SCOTT.

   Thus, once, long since, the daring of my youth
Drew nigh thy greatness with a little thing;
And thou didst take me in: thy home of truth
   Has domed me since, a heaven of sheltering,
Uplighted by the tenderness and grace
Which round thy absolute friendship ever fling

   A radiant atmosphere. Turn not thy face
From that small part of earnest thanks, I pray,
Which, spoken, leaves much more in speechless case.
   I saw thee as a strong man on his way!
Up the great peaks: I know thee stronger still;
Thy intellect unrivalled in its sway,
   Upheld and ordered by a regnant will;
While Wisdom, seer and priest of holy Fate,
Searches all truths, its prophecy to fill:
   Yet, O my friend, throned in thy heart so great,
High Love is queen, and hath no equal mate.
   May, 1857.

WERE I A SKILFUL PAINTER.

   Were I a skilful painter,
My pencil, not my pen,
Should try to teach thee hope and fear;
And who should blame me then?
Fear of the tide-like darkness
That followeth close behind,
And hope to make thee journey on
In the journey of the mind.
   Were I a skilful painter,
What should my painting be?
A tiny spring-bud peeping forth
From a withered wintry tree.
The warm blue sky of summer
Above the mountain snow,
Whence water in an infant stream,
Is trying how to flow.
   The dim light of a beacon
Upon a stormy sea,
Where wild waves, ruled by wilder winds,
Yet call themselves the free.
One sunbeam faintly gleaming
Athwart a sullen cloud,
Like dawning peace upon a brow
In angry weeping bowed.
   Morn climbing o'er the mountain,
While the vale is full of night,
And a wanderer, looking for the east,
Rejoicing in the sight.
A taper burning dimly
Amid the dawning grey,
And a maiden lifting up her head,
And lo, the coming day!

And thus, were I a painter,
My pencil, not my pen,
Should try to teach thee hope and fear;
And who should blame me then?
Fear of the tide-like darkness
That followeth close behind,
And hope to make thee journey on
In the journey of the mind.

IF I WERE A MONK, AND THOU WERT A NUN.

If I were a monk, and thou wert a nun,
   Pacing it wearily, wearily,
From chapel to cell till day were done,
   Wearily, wearily,
Oh! how would it be with these hearts of ours,
That need the sunshine, and smiles, and flowers?
   To prayer, to prayer, at the matins' call,
     Morning foul or fair;
Such prayer as from lifeless lips may fall—
     Words, but hardly prayer;
Vainly trying the thoughts to raise,
Which, in the sunshine, would burst in praise.
   Thou, in the glory of cloudless noon,
     The God revealing,
Turning thy face from the boundless boon,
     Painfully kneeling;
Or in thy chamber's still solitude,
Bending thy head o'er the legend rude.
   I, in a cool and lonely nook,
     Gloomily, gloomily,
Poring over some musty book,
     Thoughtfully, thoughtfully;
Or on the parchment margin unrolled,
Painting quaint pictures in purple and gold.
   Perchance in slow procession to meet,
     Wearily, wearily,
In an antique, narrow, high-gabled street,
     Wearily, wearily;
Thy dark eyes lifted to mine, and then
Heavily sinking to earth again.
   Sunshine and air! warmness and spring!
     Merrily, merrily!
Back to its cell each weary thing,
     Wearily, wearily!
And the heart so withered, and dry, and old,
Most at home in the cloister cold.

Thou on thy knees at the vespers' call,
   Wearily, wearily;
I looking up on the darkening wall,
   Wearily, wearily;
The chime so sweet to the boat at sea,
Listless and dead to thee and me!
  Then to the lone couch at death of day,
   Wearily, wearily;
Rising at midnight again to pray,
   Wearily, wearily;
And if through the dark those eyes looked in,
Sending them far as a thought of sin.
  And then, when thy spirit was passing away,
   Dreamily, dreamily;
The earth-born dwelling returning to clay,
   Sleepily, sleepily;
Over thee held the crucified Best,
But no warm face to thy cold cheek pressed.
  And when my spirit was passing away,
   Dreamily, dreamily;
The grey head lying 'mong ashes grey,
   Sleepily, sleepily;
No hovering angel-woman above,
Waiting to clasp me in deathless love.
  But now, beloved, thy hand in mine,
   Peacefully, peacefully;
My arm around thee, my lips on thine,
   Lovingly, lovingly,—
Oh! is not a better thing to us given
Than wearily going alone to heaven?

BLESSED ARE THE MEEK, FOR THEY SHALL INHERIT THE EARTH.

  A quiet heart, submissive, meek,
   Father do thou bestow;
Which more than granted will not seek
  To have, or give, or know.
  Each green hill then will hold its gift
   Forth to my joying eyes;
The mountains blue will then uplift
  My spirit to the skies.
  The falling water then will sound
   As if for me alone;
Nay, will not blessing more abound
  That many hear its tone?
  The trees their murmuring forth will send,
   The birds send forth their song;

The waving grass its tribute lend,
  Sweet music to prolong.
    The water-lily's shining cup,
    The trumpet of the bee,
The thousand odours floating up,
  The many-shaded sea;
    The rising sun's imprinted tread
    Upon the eastward waves;
The gold and blue clouds over head;
  The weed from far sea-caves;
    All lovely things from south to north,
    All harmonies that be,
Each will its soul of joy send forth
  To enter into me.
    And thus the wide earth I shall hold,
    A perfect gift of thine;
Richer by these, a thousandfold,
  Than if broad lands were mine.

THE HILLS.

  Behind my father's house there lies
    A little grassy brae,
Whose face my childhood's busy feet
  Ran often up in play,
Whence on the chimneys I looked down
  In wonderment alway.
  Around the house, where'er I turned,
    Great hills closed up the view;
The town 'midst their converging roots
  Was clasped by rivers two;
From one hill to another sprang
  The sky's great arch of blue.
  Oh! how I loved to climb their sides,
    And in the heather lie;
The bridle on my arm did hold
  The pony feeding by;
Beneath, the silvery streams; above,
  The white clouds in the sky.
  And now, in wandering about,
    Whene'er I see a hill,
A childish feeling of delight
  Springs in my bosom still;
And longings for the high unknown
  Follow and flow and fill.
  For I am always climbing hills,
    And ever passing on,
Hoping on some high mountain peak

To find my Father's throne;
For hitherto I've only found
His footsteps in the stone.
And in my wanderings I have met
A spirit child like me,
Who laid a trusting hand in mine,
So fearlessly and free,
That so together we have gone,
Climbing continually.
Upfolded in a spirit bud,
The child appeared in space,
Not born amid the silent hills,
But in a busy place;
And yet in every hill we see
A strange, familiar face.
For they are near our common home;
And so in trust we go,
Climbing and climbing on and on,
Whither we do not know;
Not waiting for the mournful dark,
But for the dawning slow.
Clasp my hand closer yet, my child,—
A long way we have come!
Clasp my hand closer yet, my child,—
For we have far to roam,
Climbing and climbing, till we reach
Our Heavenly Father's home.

I KNOW WHAT BEAUTY IS.

I know what beauty is, for Thou
Hast set the world within my heart;
Its glory from me will not part;
I never loved it more than now.
I know the Sabbath afternoon:
The light lies sleeping on the graves;
Against the sky the poplar waves;
The river plays a Sabbath tune.
Ah, know I not the spring's snow-bell?
The summer woods at close of even?
Autumn, when earth dies into heaven,
And winter's storms, I know them well.
I know the rapture music brings,
The power that dwells in ordered tones,
A living voice that loves and moans,
And speaks unutterable things.
Consenting beauties in a whole;
The living eye, the imperial head,

The gait of inward music bred,
The woman form, a radiant soul.
  And splendours all unspoken bide
  Within the ken of spirit's eye;
  And many a glory saileth by,
Borne on the Godhead's living tide.
  But I leave all, thou man of woe!
  Put off my shoes, and come to Thee;
  Thou art most beautiful to me;
More wonderful than all I know.
  As child forsakes his favourite toy,
  His sisters' sport, his wild bird's nest;
  And climbing to his mother's breast,
Enjoys yet more his former joy—
  I lose to find. On forehead wide
  The jewels tenfold light afford:
  So, gathered round thy glory, Lord,
All beauty else is glorified.

I WOULD I WERE A CHILD.

  I would I were a child,
That I might look, and laugh, and say, My Father!
And follow Thee with running feet, or rather
  Be led thus through the wild.
  How I would hold thy hand!
My glad eyes often to thy glory lifting,
Which casts all beauteous shadows, ever shifting,
  Over this sea and land.
  If a dark thing came near,
I would but creep within thy mantle's folding,
Shut my eyes close, thy hand yet faster holding,
  And so forget my fear.
  O soul, O soul, rejoice!
Thou art God's child indeed, for all thy sinning;
A trembling child, yet his, and worth the winning
  With gentle eyes and voice.
  The words like echoes flow.
They are too good; mine I can call them never;
Such water drinking once, I should feel ever
  As I had drunk but now.
  And yet He said it so;
'Twas He who taught our child-lips to say, Father!
Like the poor youth He told of, that did gather
  His goods to him, and go.
  Ah! Thou dost lead me, God;
But it is dark; no stars; the way is dreary;

Almost I sleep, I am so very weary
　Upon this rough hill-road.
　　Almost! Nay, I *do* sleep.
There is no darkness save in this my dreaming;
Thy Fatherhood above, around, is beaming;
　Thy hand my hand doth keep.
　　This torpor one sun-gleam
Would break. My soul hath wandered into sleeping;
Dream-shades oppress; I call to Thee with weeping,
　Wake me from this my dream.
　　And as a man doth say,
Lo! I do dream, yet trembleth as he dreameth;
While dim and dream-like his true history seemeth,
　Lost in the perished day;
　　(For heavy, heavy night
Long hours denies the day) so this dull sorrow
Upon my heart, but half believes a morrow
　Will ever bring thy light.
　　God, art Thou in the room?
Come near my bed; oh! draw aside the curtain;
A child's heart would say *Father*, were it certain
　That it did not presume.
　　But if this dreary bond
I may not break, help Thou thy helpless sleeper;
Resting in Thee, my sleep will sink the deeper,
　All evil dreams beyond.
　　Father! I dare at length.
My childhood, thy gift, all my claim in speaking;
Sinful, yet hoping, I to Thee come, seeking
　Thy tenderness, my strength.
　　THE LOST SOUL.
　Brothers, look there!
　What! see ye nothing yet?
Knit your eyebrows close, and stare;
Send your souls forth in the gaze,
As my finger-point is set,
Through the thick of the foggy air.
Beyond the air, you see the dark;
(For the darkness hedges still our ways;)
And beyond the dark, oh, lives away!
Dim and far down, surely you mark
A huge world-heap of withered years
Dropt from the boughs of eternity?
See ye not something lying there,
Shapeless as a dumb despair,
Yet a something that spirits can recognise

With the vision dwelling in their eyes?
It hath the form of a man!
As a huge moss-rock in a valley green,
When the light to freeze began,
Thickening with crystals of dark between,
Might look like a sleeping man.
What think ye it, brothers? I know it well.
I know by your eyes ye see it—tell.
   'Tis a poor lost soul, alack!
It was alive some ages back;
One that had wings and might have had eyes
I think I have heard that he wrote a book;
But he gathered his life up into a nook,
And perished amid his own mysteries,
Which choked him, because he had not faith,
But was proud in the midst of sayings dark
Which God had charactered on his walls;
And the light which burned up at intervals,
To be spent in reading what God saith,
He lazily trimmed it to a spark,
And then it went out, and his soul was dark.
    Is there aught between thee and me,
  Soul, that art lying there?
  Is any life yet left in thee,
  So that thou couldst but spare
  A word to reveal the mystery
  Of the banished from light and air?
    Alas, O soul! thou wert once
  As the soul that cries to thee!
Thou hadst thy place in the mystic dance
From the doors of the far eternity,
Issuing still with feet that glance
To the music of the free!
    Alas! O soul, to think
That thou wert made like me!
With a heart for love, and a thirst to drink
From the wells that feed the sea!
And with hands of truth to have been a link
'Twixt mine and the parent knee;
And with eyes to pierce to the further brink
Of things I cannot see!
    Alas, alas, my brother!
To thee my heart is drawn:
My soul had been such another,
In the dark amidst the dawn!

As a child in the eyes of its mother
Dead on the flowery lawn!
  I mourn for thee, poor friend!
A spring from a cliff did drop:
To drink by the wayside God would bend,
And He found thee a broken cup!
He threw thee aside, His way to wend
Further and higher up.
    Alack! sad soul, alack!
As if I lay in thy grave,
I feel the Infinite sucking back
The individual life it gave.
Thy spring died to a pool, deep, black,
Which the sun from its pit did lave.
    Thou might'st have been one of us,
Cleaving the storm and fire;
Aspiring through faith to the glorious,
Higher and ever higher;
Till the world of storms look tremulous,
Far down, like a smitten lyre!
    A hundred years! he might
Have darted through the gloom,
Like that swift angel that crossed our flight
Where the thunder-cloud did loom,
From his upcast pinions flashing the light
Of some inward word or doom.
  It heareth not, brothers, the terrible thing!
Sounds no sense to its ear will bring.
Hath God forgotten it, alas!
Lost in eternity's lumber room?
Will the wave of his Spirit never pass
Over it through the insensate gloom?
It lies alone in its lifeless world,
As a frozen bud on the earth lies curled;
Sightless and soundless, without a cry,
On the flat of its own vacuity.
   Up, brothers, up! for a storm is nigh;
We will smite the wing up the steepest sky;
Through the rushing air
We will climb the stair
That to heaven from the vaults doth leap;
We will measure its height
By the strokes of our flight,
Its span by the tempest's sweep.
What matter the hail or the clashing winds!
We know by the tempest we do not lie

Dead in the pits of eternity.
Brothers, let us be strong in our minds,
Lest the storm should beat us back,
Or the treacherous calm sink from beneath our wings,
And lower us gently from our track
To the depths of forgotten things.
Up, brothers, up! 'tis the storm or we!
'Tis the storm or God for the victory!
   A DREAM WITHIN A DREAM.
   THE OUTER DREAM.
   Young, as the day's first-born Titanic brood,
Lifting their foreheads jubilant to heaven,
Rose the great mountains on my opening dream.
And yet the aged peace of countless years
Reposed on every crag and precipice
Outfacing ruggedly the storms that swept
Far overhead the sheltered furrow-vales;
Which smiled abroad in green as the clouds broke
Drifting adown the tide of the wind-waves,
Till shattered on the mountain rocks. Oh! still,
And cold and hard to look upon, like men
Who do stern deeds in times of turbulence,
Quell the hail-rattle with their granite brows,
And let the thunder burst and pass away—
They too did gather round sky-dwelling peaks
The trailing garments of the travelling sun,
Which he had lifted from his ocean-bed,
And swept along his road. They rent them down
In scattering showers upon the trees and grass,
In noontide rains with heavy ringing drops,
Or in still twilight moisture tenderly.
And from their sides were born the gladsome streams;
Some creeping gently out in tiny springs,
As they were just created, scarce a foot
From the hill's surface, in the matted roots
Of plants, whose green betrays the secret birth;
Some hurrying forth from caverns deep and dark,
Upfilling to the brim a basin huge,
Thick covered with soft moss, greening the wave,
As evermore it welled over the edge
Upon the rocks below in boiling heaps;
Fit basin for a demi-god at morn,
Waking amid the crags, to lave his limbs,
Then stride, Hyperion, o'er sun-paven peaks.
And down the hill-side sped the fresh-born wave,
Now hid from sight in arched caverns cold,

Now arrowing slantwise down the terraced steep,
Now springing like a child from step to step
Of the rough water-stair; until it found
A deep-hewn passage for its slower course,
Guiding it down to lowliness and rest,
Betwixt wet walls of darkness, darker yet
With pine trees lining all their sides like hair,
Or as their own straight needles clothe their boughs;
Until at length in broader light it ran,
With more articulate sounds amid the stones,
In the slight shadow of the maiden birch,
And the stream-loving willow; and ere long
Great blossoming trees dropt flowers upon its breast;
Chiefly the crimson-spotted, cream-white flowers,
Heaped up in cones amid cone-drooping leaves;
Green hanging leaf-cones, towering white flower-cones
Upon the great cone-fashioned chestnut tree.
Each made a tiny ripple where it fell,
The trembling pleasure of the smiling wave,
Which bore it then, in slow funereal course,
Down to the outspread sunny sheen, where lies
The lake uplooking to the far-off snow,
Its mother still, though now so far away;
Feeding it still with long descending lines
Of shining, speeding streams, that gather peace
In journeying to the rest of that still lake
Now lying sleepy in the warm red sun,
Which says its dear goodnight, and goeth down.
   All pale, and withered, and disconsolate,
The moon is looking on impatiently;
For 'twixt the shining tent-roof of the day,
And the sun-deluged lake, for mirror-floor,
Her thin pale lamping is too sadly grey
To shoot, in silver-barbed, white-plumed arrows,
Cold maiden splendours on the flashing fish:
Wait for thy empire Night, day-weary moon!
And thou shalt lord it in one realm at least,
Where two souls walk a single Paradise.
Take to thee courage, for the sun is gone;
His praisers, the glad birds, have hid their heads;
Long, ghost-like forms of trees lie on the grass;
All things are clothed in an obscuring light,
Fusing their outline in a dreamy mass;
Some faint, dim shadows from thy beauty fall
On the clear lake which melts them half away—

Shine faster, stronger, O reviving moon!
Burn up, O lamp of Earth, hung high in Heaven!
   And through a warm thin summer mist she shines,
A silver setting to the diamond stars;
And the dark boat cleaveth a glittering way,
Where the one steady beauty of the moon
Makes many changing beauties on the wave
Broken by jewel-dropping oars, which drive
The boat, as human impulses the soul;
While, like the sovereign will, the helm's firm law
Directs the whither of the onward force.
At length midway he leaves the swaying oars
Half floating in the blue gulf underneath,
And on a load of gathered flowers reclines,
Leaving the boat to any air that blows,
His soul to any pulse from the unseen heart.
Straight from the helm a white hand gleaming flits,
And settles on his face, and nestles there,
Pale, night-belated butterfly, to sleep.
For on her knees his head lies satisfied;
And upward, downward, dark eyes look and rest,
Finding their home in likeness. Lifting then
Her hair upon her white arm heavily,
The overflowing of her beauteousness,
Her hand that cannot trespass, singles out
Some of the curls that stray across her lap;
And mingling dark locks in the pallid light,
She asks him which is darker of the twain,
Which his, which hers, and laugheth like a lute.
But now her hair, an unvexed cataract,
Falls dark and heavy round his upturned face,
And with a heaven shuts out the shallow sky,
A heaven profound, the home of two black stars;
Till, tired with gazing, face to face they lie,
Suspended, with closed eyelids, in the night;
Their bodies bathed in conscious sleepiness,
While o'er their souls creeps every rippling breath
Of the night-gambols of the moth-winged wind,
Flitting a handbreadth, folding up its wings,
Its dreamy wings, then spreading them anew,
And with an unfelt gliding, like the years,
Wafting them to a water-lily bed,
Whose shield-like leaves and chalice-bearing arms
Hold back the boat from the slow-sloping shore,
Far as a child might shoot with his toy-bow.
There the long drooping grass drooped to the wave;

And, ever as the moth-wind lit thereon,
A small-leafed tree, whose roots were always cool,
Dipped one low bow, with many sister-leaves,
Upon the water's face with a low plash,
Lifting and dipping yet and yet again;
And aye the water-drops rained from the leaves,
With music-laughter as they found their home.
And from the woods came blossom-fragrance, faint,
Or full, like rising, falling harmonies;
Luxuriance of life, which overflows
In scents ethereal on the ocean air;
Each breathing on the rest the blessedness
Of its peculiar being, filled with good
Till its cup runneth over with delight:
They drank the mingled odours as they lay,
The air in which the sensuous being breathes,
Till summer-sleep fell on their hearts and eyes.
   The night was mild and innocent of ill;
'Twas but a sleeping day that breathed low,
And babbled in its sleep. The moon at length
Grew sleepy too. Her level glances crept
Through sleeping branches to their curtained eyes,
As down the steep bank of the west she slid,
Slowly and slowly
           But alas! alas!
The awful time 'twixt moondown and sunrise!
It is a ghostly time. A low thick fog
Steamed up and swathed the trees, and overwhelmed
The floating couch with pall on pall of grey.
The sky was desolate, dull, and meaningless.
The blazing hues of the last sunset eve,
And the pale magic moonshine that had made
The common, strange,—all were swept clean away;
The earth around, the great sky over, were
Like a deserted theatre, tomb-dumb;
The lights long dead; the first sick grey of morn
Oozing through rents in the slow-mouldering curtain;
The sweet sounds fled away for evermore;
Nought left, except a creeping chill, a sense
As if dead deeds were strown upon the stage,
As if dead bodies simulated life,
And spoke dead words without informing thought.
A horror, as of power without a soul,
Dark, undefined, and mighty unto ill,
Jarred through the earth and through the vault-like air.

And on the sleepers fell a wondrous dream,
That dured till sunrise, filling all the cells
Remotest of the throbbing heart and brain.
And as I watched them, ever and anon
The quivering limb and half-unclosèd eye
Witnessed of torture scarce endured, and yet
Endured; for still the dream had mastery,
And held them in a helplessness supine;
Till, by degrees, the labouring breath grew calm,
Save frequent murmured sighs; and o'er each face
Stole radiant sadness, and a hopeful grief;
And the convulsive motion passed away.
  Upon their faces, reading them, I gazed,—
Reading them earnestly, like wondrous book,—
When suddenly the vapours of the dream
Rose and enveloped me, and through my soul
Passed with possession; will fell fast asleep.
And through the portals of the spirit-land,
Upon whose frontiers time and space grow dumb,
Quenched like a cloud that all the roaring wind
Drives not beyond the mountain top, I went,
And entering, beheld them in their dream.
Their world inwrapt me for the time as mine,
And what befel them there, I saw, and tell.

THE INNER DREAM.

It was a drizzly morning where I stood.
The cloud had sunk, and filled with fold on fold
The chimneyed city; so the smoke rose not,
But spread diluted in the cloud, and fell
A black precipitate on miry streets,
Where dim grey faces vision-like went by,
But half-awake, half satisfied with sleep.
  Slave engines had begun their ceaseless growl
Of labour. Iron bands and huge stone blocks
That held them to their task, strained, shook, until
The city trembled. Those pale-visaged forms
Were hastening on to feed their groaning strength
With labour to the full.
              Look! there they come,
Poor amid poverty; she with her gown
Drawn over her meek head; he trying much,
But fruitless half, to shield her from the rain.
They enter the wide gates, amid the jar,
And clash, and shudder of the awful force
That, conquering force, still vibrates on, as if
With an excess of power, hungry for work.

With differing strength to different tasks they part,
To be the soul of knowledge unto strength;
For man has eked his body out with wheels,
And cranks, and belts, and levers, pinions, screws—
One body all, pervaded still with life
From man the maker's will. 'Mid keen-eyed men,
Thin featured and exact, his part is found;
Hers where the dusk air shines with lustrous eyes.
   And there they laboured through the murky day,
Whose air was livid mist, their only breath;
Foul floating dust of swift revolving wheels
And feathery spoil of fast contorted threads
Making a sultry chaos in the sun.
Until at length slow swelled the welcome dark,
A dull Lethean heaving tide of death,
Up from the caves of Night to make an end;
And filling every corner of the place,
Choked in its waves the clanking of the looms.
And Earth put on her sleeping dress, and took
Her children home into its bosom-folds,
And nursed them as a mother-ghost might sit
With her neglected darlings in the dark.
So with dim satisfaction in their hearts,
Though with tired feet and aching head, they went,
Parting the clinging fog to find their home.
It was a dreary place. Unfinished walls,
Far drearier than ruins overspread
With long-worn sweet forgetfulness, amidst
Earth-heaps and bricks, rain-pools and ugliness,
Rose up around, banishing further yet
The Earth, with its spring-time, young-mother smile,
From children's eyes that had forgot to play.
But though the house was dull and wrapt in fog,
It yet awoke to life, yea, cheerfulness,
When darkness oped a fire-eye in the grate,
And the dim candle's smoky flame revealed
A room which could not be all desolate,
Being a temple, proven by the signs
Seen in the ancient place. For here was light;
And blazing fire with darkness on its skirts;
Bread; and pure water, ready to make clean,
Beside a chest of holiday attire;
And in the twilight edges of the light,
A book scarce seen; and for the wondrous veil,
Those human forms, behind which lay concealed
The Holy of Holies, God's own secret place,

The lowly human heart wherein He dwells.
And by the table-altar they sat down
To eat their Eucharist, God feeding them:
Their food was Love, made visible in Form—
Incarnate Love in food. For he to whom
A common meal can be no Eucharist,
Who thanks for food and strength, not for the love
That made cold water for its blessedness,
And wine for gladness' sake, has yet to learn
The heart-delight of inmost thankfulness
For innermost reception.
           Then they sat
Resting with silence, the soul's inward sleep,
Which feedeth it with strength; till gradually
They grew aware of light, that overcame
The light within, and through the dingy blind,
Cast from the window-frame, two shadow-glooms
That made a cross of darkness on the white,
Dark messenger of light itself unseen.
The woman rose, and half she put aside
The veil that hid the whole of glorious night;
And lo! a wind had mowed the earth-sprung fog;
And lo! on high the white exultant moon
From clear blue window curtained all with white,
Greeted them, at their shadowy window low,
With quiet smile; for two things made her glad:
One that she saw the glory of the sun;
For while the earth lay all athirst for light,
She drank the fountain-waves. The other joy;
Sprung from herself: she fought the darkness well,
Thinning the great cone-shadow of the earth,
Paling its ebon hue with radiant showers
Upon its sloping side. The woman said,
With hopeful look: "To-morrow will be bright
With sunshine for our holiday—to-morrow—
Think! we shall see the green fields in the sun."
So with hearts hoping for a simple joy,
Yet high withal, being no less than the sun,
They laid them down in nightly death that waits
Patiently for the day.
           That sun was high
When they awoke at length. The moon, low down,
Had almost vanished, clothed upon with light;
And night was swallowed up of day. In haste,
Chiding their weariness that leagued with sleep,
They, having clothed themselves in clean attire,

By the low door, stooping with priestly hearts,
Entered God's vision-room, his wonder-world.
   One side the street, the windows all were moons
To light the other that in shadow lay.
The path was almost dry; the wind asleep.
And down the sunny side a woman came
In a red cloak that made the whole street glad—
Fit clothing, though she was so feeble and old;
For when they stopped and asked her how she fared,
She said with cheerful words, and smile that owed
None of its sweetness to an ivory lining:
"I'm always better in the open air."
"Dear heart!" said they, "how freely she will breathe
In the open air of heaven!" She stood in the morn
Like a belated autumn-flower in spring,
Dazed by the rushing of the new-born life
Up the earth's winding cavern-stairs to see
Through window-buds the calling, waking sun.
Or as in dreams we meet the ghost of one
Beloved in youth, who walketh with few words,
And they are of the past. Yet, joy to her!
She too from earthy grave was climbing up
Unto the spirit-windows high and far,
She the new life for a celestial spring,
Answering the light that shineth evermore.
   With hopeful sadness thus they passed along
Dissolving streets towards the smiles of spring,
Of which green visions gleamed and glided by,
Across far-narrowing avenues of brick:
The ripples only of her laughter float
Through the low winding caverns of the town;
Yet not a stone upon the paven street,
But shareth in the impulse of her joy,
Heaven's life that thrills anew through the outworn earth;
Descending like the angel that did stir
Bethesda's pool, and made the sleepy wave
Pulse with quick healing through the withered limb,
In joyous pangs. By an unfinished street,
Forth came they on a wide and level space;
Green fields lay side by side, and hedgerow trees
Stood here and there as waiting for some good.
But no calm river meditated through
The weary flat to the less level sea;
No forest trees on pillared stems and boughs
Bent in great Gothic arches, bore aloft
A cloudy temple-roof of tremulous leaves;

No clear line where the kissing lips of sky
And earth meet undulating, but a haze
That hides—oh, if it hid wild waves! alas!
It hides but fields, it hides but fields and trees!
Save eastward, where a few hills, far away,
Came forth in the sun, or drew back when the clouds
Went over them, dissolving them in shade.
But the life-robe of earth was beautiful,
As all most common things are loveliest;
A forest of green waving fairy trees,
That carpeted the earth for lowly feet,
Bending unto their tread, lowliest of all
Earth's lowly children born for ministering
Unto the heavenly stranger, stately man;
That he, by subtle service from all kinds,
From every breeze and every bounding wave,
From night-sky cavernous with heaps of storm,
And from the hill rejoicing in the sun,
Might grow a humble, lowly child of God;
Lowly, as knowing his high parentage;
Humble, because all beauties wait on him,
Like lady-servants ministering for love.
And he that hath not rock, and hill, and stream,
Must learn to look for other beauty near;
To know the face of ocean solitudes,
The darkness dashed with glory, and the shades
Wind-fretted, and the mingled tints upthrown
From shallow bed, or raining from the sky.
And he that hath not ocean, and dwells low,
Not hill-befriended, if his eyes have ceased
To drink enjoyment from the billowy grass,
And from the road-side flower (like one who dwells
With homely features round him every day,
And so takes refuge in the loving eyes
Which are their heaven, the dwelling-place of light),
Must straightway lift his eyes unto the heavens,
Like God's great palette, where His artist hand
Never can strike the brush, but beauty wakes;
Vast sweepy comet-curves, that net the soul
In pleasure; endless sky-stairs; patient clouds,
White till they blush at the sun's goodnight kiss;
And filmy pallours, and great mountain crags.
But beyond all, absorbing all the rest,
Lies the great heaven, the expression of deep space,
Foreshortened to a vaulted dome of blue;
The Infinite, crowded in a single glance,

Where yet the eye descends depth within depth;
Like mystery of Truth, clothed in high form,
Evasive, spiritual, no limiting,
But something that denies an end, and yet
Can be beheld by wondering human eyes.
There looking up, one well may feel how vain
To search for God in this vast wilderness!
For over him would arch void depth for ever;
Nor ever would he find a God or Heaven,
Though lifting wings were his to soar abroad
Through boundless heights of space; or eyes to dive
To microscopic depths: he would come back,
And say, *There is no God;* and sit and weep;
Till in his heart a child's voice woke and cried,
Father! my Father! Then the face of God
Breaks forth with eyes, everywhere, suddenly
And not a space of blue, nor floating cloud,
Nor grassy vale, nor distant purple height,
But, trembling with a presence all divine,
Says, *Here I am, my child.*
                        Gazing awhile,
They let the lesson of the sky sink deep
Into their hearts; withdrawing then their eyes,
They knew the Earth again. And as they went,
Oft in the changing heavens, those distant hills
Shone clear upon the horizon. Then awoke
A strange and unknown longing in their souls,
As if for something loved in years gone by,
And vanished in its beauty and its love
So long, that it retained no name or form,
And lay on childhood's verge, all but forgot,
Wrapt in the enchanted rose-mists of that land:
As if amidst those hills were wooded dells,
Summer, and gentle winds, and odours free,
Deep sleeping waters, gorgeous flowers, and birds,
Pure winged throats. But here, all things around
Were in their spring. The very light that lay
Upon the grass seemed new-born like the grass,
Sprung with it from the earth. The very stones
Looked warm. The brown ploughed earth seemed swelling up,
Filled like a sponge with sunbeams, which lay still,
Nestling unseen, and broodingly, and warm,
In every little nest, corner, or crack,
Wherein might hide a blind and sleepy seed,
Waiting the touch of penetrative life
To wake, and grow, and beautify the earth.

The mossy stems and boughs, where yet no life
Exuberant overflowed in buds and leaves,
Were clothed in golden splendours, interwoven
With many shadows from the branches bare.
And through their tops the west wind rushing went,
Calling aloud the sleeping sap within:
The thrill passed downwards from the roots in air
To the roots tremulous in the embracing ground.
And though no buds with little dots of light
Sparkled the darkness of the hedgerow twigs;
Softening, expanding in the warm light-bath,
Seemed the dry smoky bark.
    Thus in the fields
They spent their holiday. And when the sun
Was near the going down, they turned them home
With strengthened hearts. For they were filled with light,
And with the spring; and, like the bees, went back
To their dark house, laden with blessed sights,
With gladsome sounds home to their treasure-cave;
Where henceforth sudden gleams of spring would pass
Thorough the four-walled darkness of the room;
And sounds of spring-time whisper trembling by,
Though stony streets with iron echoed round.
And as they crossed a field, they came by chance
Upon a place where once a home had been;
Fragments of ruined walls, half-overgrown
With moss, for even stones had their green robe.
It had been a small cottage, with a plot
Of garden-ground in front, mapped out with walks
Now scarce discernible, but that the grass
Was thinner, the ground harder to the foot:
The place was simply shadowed with an old
Almost erased human carefulness.
Close by the ruined wall, where once had been
The door dividing it from the great world,
Making it *home*, a single snowdrop grew.
'Twas the sole remnant of a family
Of flowers that in this garden once had dwelt,
Vanished with all their hues of glowing life,
Save one too white for death.
    And as its form
Arose within the brain, a feeling sprung
Up in their souls, new, white, and delicate;
A waiting, longing, patient hopefulness,
The snowdrop of the heart. The heavenly child,
Pale with the earthly cold, hung its meek head,

Enduring all, and so victorious;
The Summer's earnest in the waking Earth,
The spirit's in the heart.
                    I love thee, flower,
With a love almost human, tenderly;
The Spring's first child, yea, thine, my hoping heart!
Upon thy inner leaves and in thy heart,
Enough of green to tell thou know'st the grass;
In thy white mind remembering lowly friends;
But most I love thee for that little stain
Of earth on thy transfigured radiancy,
Which thou hast lifted with thee from thy grave,
The soiling of thy garments on thy road,
Travelling forth into the light and air,
The heaven of thy pure rest. Some gentle rain
Will surely wash thee white, and send the earth
Back to the place of earth; but now it signs
Thee child of earth, of human birth as we.
   With careful hands uprooting it, they bore
The little plant a willing captive home;
Willing to enter dark abodes, secure
In its own tale of light. As once of old,
Bearing all heaven in words of promising,
The Angel of the Annunciation came,
It carried all the spring into that house;
A pot of mould its only tie to Earth,
Its heaven an ell of blue 'twixt chimney-tops,
Its world henceforth that little, low-ceiled room,
Symbol and child of spring, it took its place
'Midst all those types, to be a type with them,
Of what so many feel, not knowing it;
The hidden springtime that is drawing nigh.
And henceforth, when the shadow of the cross
Will enter, clothed in moonlight, still and dark,
The flower will nestle at its foot till day,
Pale, drooping, heart-content.
                    To rest they went.
And all night long the snowdrop glimmered white
Amid the dark, unconscious and unseen.
   Before the sun had crowned his eastern hill
With its world-diadem, they woke.
                    I looked
Out of the windows of the inner dream,
And saw the edge of the sun's glory rise
Eastward behind the hills, the lake-cup's rim.
And as it came, it sucked up in itself,

As deeds drink words, or daylight candle-flame,
That other sun rising to light the dream.
They lay awake and thoughtful, comforted
With yesterday which nested in their hearts,
Yet haunted with the sound of grinding wheels.
THE OUTER DREAM.
  And as they lay and looked into the room,
It wavered, changed, dissolved beneath the sun,
Which mingled both the mornings in their eyes,
Till the true conquered, and the unreal passed.
No walls, but woods bathed in a level sun;
No ceiling, but the vestal sky of morn;
No bed, but flowers floating 'mid floating leaves
On water which grew audible as they stirred
And lifted up their heads. And a low wind
That flowed from out the west, washed from their eye
The last films of the dream. And they sat up,
Silent for one long cool delicious breath,
Gazing upon each other lost and found,
With a dumb ecstasy, new, undefined.
Followed a long embrace, and then the oars
Broke up their prison-bands.
                    And through the woods
They slowly went, beneath a firmament
Of boughs, and clouded leaves, filmy and pale
In the sunshine, but shadowy on the grass.
And roving odours met them on their way,
Sun-quickened odours, which the fog had slain.
And their green sky had many a blossom-moon,
And constellations thick with starry flowers.
And deep and still were all the woods, except
For the Memnonian, glory-stricken birds;
And golden beetles 'mid the shadowy roots,
Green goblins of the grass, and mining mice;
And on the leaves the fairy butterflies,
Or doubting in the air, scarlet and blue.
The divine depth of summer clasped the Earth.
  But 'twixt their hearts and summer's perfectness
Came a dividing thought that seemed to say:
"*Ye wear strange looks.*" Did summer speak, or they?
They said within: "We know that ye are fair,
Bright flowers; but ye shine far away, as in
A land of other thoughts. Alas! alas!
  "Where shall we find the snowdrop-bell half-blown?
What shall we do? we feel the throbbing spring
Bursting in new and unexpressive thoughts;

Our hearts are swelling like a tied-up bud,
And summer crushes them with too much light.
Action is bubbling up within our souls;
The woods oppress us more than stony streets;
That was the life indeed; this is the dream;
Summer is too complete for growing hearts;
They need a broken season, and a land
With shadows pointing ever far away;
Where incompleteness rouses longing thoughts
With spires abrupt, and broken spheres, and circles
Cut that they may be widened evermore:
Through shattered cloudy roof, looks in the sky,
A discord from a loftier harmony;
And tempests waken peace within our thoughts,
Driving them inward to the inmost rest.
Come, my beloved, we will haste and go
To those pale faces of our fellow men;
Our loving hearts, burning with summer-fire,
Will cast a glow upon their pallidness;
Our hands will help them, far as servants may;
Hands are apostles still to saviour-hearts.
So we may share their blessedness with them;
So may the snowdrop time be likewise ours;
And Earth smile tearfully the spirit smile
Wherewith she smiled upon our holiday,
As a sweet child may laugh with weeping eyes.
If ever we return, these glorious flowers
May all be snowdrops of a higher spring."
Their eyes one moment met, and then they knew
That they did mean the same thing in their hearts.
So with no farther words they turned and went
Back to the boat, and so across the mere.
  I wake from out my dream, and know my room,
My darling books, the cherub forms above;
I know 'tis springtime in the world without;
I feel it springtime in my world within;
I know that bending o'er an early flower,
Crocus, or primrose, or anemone,
The heart that striveth for a higher life,
And hath not yet been conquered, findeth there
A beauty deep, unshared by any rose,
A human loveliness about the flower;
That a heath-bell upon a lonely waste
Hath more than scarlet splendour on thick leaves;
That a blue opening 'midst rain-bosomed clouds
Is more than Paphian sun-set harmonies;

That higher beauty dwells on earth, because
Man seeks a higher home than Paradise;
And, having lost, is roused thereby to fill
A deeper need than could be filled by all
The lost ten times restored; and so he loves
The snowdrop more than the magnolia;
Spring-hope is more to him than summer-joy;
Dark towns than Eden-groves with rivers four.

AFTER AN OLD LEGEND.

The monk was praying in his cell,
  And he did pray full sore;
He had been praying on his knees
  For two long hours and more.
  And in the midst, and suddenly,
  He felt his eyes ope wide;
And he lifted not his head, but saw
  A man's feet him beside.
  And almost to his feet there reached
  A garment strangely knit;
Some woman's fingers, ages agone,
  Had trembled, in making it.
  The monk's eyes went up the garment,
  Until a hand they spied;
A cut from a chisel was on it,
  And another scar beside.
  Then his eyes sprang to the face
  With a single thirsty bound;
'Twas He, and he nigh had fainted;
  His eyes had the Master found.
  On his ear fell the convent bell,
  That told him the poor did wait
For his hand to divide the daily bread,
  All at the convent-gate.
  And a storm of thoughts within him
  Blew hither and thither long;
And the bell kept calling all the time
  With its iron merciless tongue.
  He looked in the Master's eyes,
  And he sprang to his feet in strength:
"Though I find him not when I come back,
  I shall find him the more at length."
  He went, and he fed the poor,
  All at the convent-gate;
And like one bereft, with heavy feet
  Went back to be desolate.

He stood by the door, unwilling
  To see the cell so bare;
He opened the door, and lo!
  The Master was standing there.
  "I have waited for thee, because
  The poor had not to wait;
And I stood beside thee all the time,
  In the crowd at the convent-gate."
  * * * * *
  But it seems to me, though the story
  Sayeth no word of this,
If the monk had stayed, the Lord would have stayed,
  Nor crushed that heart of his.
  For out of the far-off times
  A word sounds tenderly:
"The poor ye have always with you,
  And ye have not always me."

THE TREE'S PRAYER.

  Alas! 'tis cold and dark;
The wind all night has sung a wintry tune;
Hail from black clouds that swallowed up the moon
  Has beat against my bark.
  Oh! when will it be spring?
The sap moves not within my withered veins;
Through all my frozen roots creep numbing pains,
  That they can hardly cling.
  The sun shone out last morn;
I felt the warmth through every fibre float;
I thought I heard a thrush's piping note,
  Of hope and sadness born.
  Then came the sea-cloud driven;
The tempest hissed through all my outstretched boughs,
Hither and thither tossed me in its snows,
  Beneath the joyless heaven.
  O for the sunny leaves!
Almost I have forgot the breath of June!
Forgot the feathery light-flakes from the moon!
  The praying summer-eves!
  O for the joyous birds,
Which are the tongues of us, mute, longing trees!
O for the billowy odours, and the bees
  Abroad in scattered herds!
  The blessing of cool showers!
The gratefulness that thrills through every shoot!
The children playing round my deep-sunk root,
  Shadowed in hot noon hours!

Alas! the cold clear dawn
Through the bare lattice-work of twigs around!
Another weary day of moaning sound
On the thin-shadowed lawn!
   Yet winter's noon is past:
I'll stretch my arms all night into the wind,
Endure all day the chill air and unkind;
My leaves *will* come at last.

A STORY OF THE SEA-SHORE.
INTRODUCTION.

   I sought the long clear twilights of the North,
When, from its nest of trees, my father's house
Sees the Aurora deepen into dawn
Far northward in the East, o'er the hill-top;
And fronts the splendours of the northern West,
Where sunset dies into that ghostly gleam
That round the horizon creepeth all the night
Back to the jubilance of gracious morn.
I found my home in homeliness unchanged;
For love that maketh home, unchangeable,
Received me to the rights of sonship still.
O vaulted summer-heaven, borne on the hills!
Once more thou didst embrace me, whom, a child,
Thy drooping fulness nourished into joy.
Once more the valley, pictured forth with sighs,
Rose on my present vision, and, behold!
In nothing had the dream bemocked the truth:
The waters ran as garrulous as before;
The wild flowers crowded round my welcome feet;
The hills arose and dwelt alone in heaven;
And all had learned new tales against I came.
Once more I trod the well-known fields with him
Whose fatherhood had made me search for God's;
And it was old and new like the wild flowers,
The waters, and the hills, but dearer far.
   Once on a day, my cousin Frank and I,
Drove on a seaward road the dear white mare
Which oft had borne me to the lonely hills.
Beside me sat a maiden, on whose face
I had not looked since we were boy and girl;
But the old friendship straightway bloomed anew.
The heavens were sunny, and the earth was green;
The harebells large, and oh! so plentiful;
While butterflies, as blue as they, danced on,
Borne purposeless on pulses of clear joy,
In sportive time to their Aeolian clang.

That day as we talked on without restraint,
Brought near by memories of days that were,
And therefore are for ever—by the joy
Of motion through a warm and shining air,
By the glad sense of freedom and like thoughts,
And by the bond of friendship with the dead,
She told the tale which I would mould anew
To a more lasting form of utterance.
   For I had wandered back to childish years;
And asked her if she knew a ruin old,
Whose masonry, descending to the waves,
Faced up the sea-cliff at whose rocky feet
The billows fell and died along the coast.
'Twas one of my child marvels. For, each year,
We turned our backs upon the ripening corn,
And sought the borders of the desert sea.
O joy of waters! mingled with the fear
Of a blind force that knew not what to do,
But spent its strength of waves in lashing aye
The rocks which laughed them into foam and flight.
   But oh, the varied riches of that port!
For almost to the beach, but that a wall
Inclosed them, reached the gardens of a lord,
His shady walks, his ancient trees of state;
His river, which, with course indefinite,
Wandered across the sands without the wall,
And lost itself in finding out the sea:
Within, it floated swans, white splendours; lay
Beneath the fairy leap of a wire bridge;
Vanished and reappeared amid the shades,
And led you where the peacock's plumy heaven
Bore azure suns with green and golden rays.
Ah! here the skies showed higher, and the clouds
More summer-gracious, filled with stranger shapes;
And when they rained, it was a golden rain
That sparkled as it fell, an odorous rain.
   But there was one dream-spot—my tale must wait
Until I tell the wonder of that spot.
It was a little room, built somehow—how
I do not know—against a steep hill-side,
Whose top was with a circular temple crowned,
Seen from far waves when winds were off the shore—
So that, beclouded, ever in the night
Of a luxuriant ivy, its low door,
Half-filled with rainbow hues of deep-stained glass,
Appeared to open right into the hill.

Never to sesame of mine that door
Yielded that room; but through one undyed pane,
Gazing with reverent curiosity,
I saw a little chamber, round and high,
Which but to see, was to escape the heat,
And bathe in coolness of the eye and brain;
For it was dark and green. Upon one side
A window, unperceived from without,
Blocked up by ivy manifold, whose leaves,
Like crowded heads of gazers, row on row,
Climbed to the top; and all the light that came
Through the thick veil was green, oh, kindest hue!
But in the midst, the wonder of the place,
Against the back-ground of the ivy bossed,
On a low column stood, white, pure, and still,
A woman-form in marble, cold and clear.
I know not what it was; it may have been
A Silence, or an Echo fainter still;
But that form yet, if form it can be called,
So undefined and pale, gleams vision-like
In the lone treasure-chamber of my soul,
Surrounded with its mystic temple dark.
   Then came the thought, too joyous to keep joy,
Turning to very sadness for relief:
To sit and dream through long hot summer days,
Shrouded in coolness and sea-murmurings,
Forgot by all till twilight shades grew dark;
And read and read in the Arabian Nights,
Till all the beautiful grew possible;
And then when I had read them every one,
To find behind the door, against the wall,
Old volumes, full of tales, such as in dreams
One finds in bookshops strange, in tortuous streets;
Beside me, over me, soul of the place,
Filling the gloom with calm delirium,
That wondrous woman-statue evermore,
White, radiant; fading, as the darkness grew,
Into a ghostly pallour, that put on,
To staring eyes, a vague and shifting form.
   But the old castle on the shattered shore—
Not the green refuge from the summer heat—
Drew forth our talk that day. For, as I said,
I asked her if she knew it. She replied,
"I know it well;" and added instantly:
"A woman used to live, my mother tells,
In one of its low vaults, so near the sea,

That in high tides and northern winds it was
No more a castle-vault, but a sea-cave!"
"I found there," I replied, "a turret stair
Leading from level of the ground above
Down to a vault, whence, through an opening square,
Half window and half loophole, you look forth
Wide o'er the sea; but the dim-sounding waves
Are many feet beneath, and shrunk in size
To a great ripple. I could tell you now
A tale I made about a little girl,
Dark-eyed and pale, with long seaweed-like hair,
Who haunts that room, and, gazing o'er the deep,
Calls it her mother, with a childish glee,
Because she knew no other." "This," said she,
"Was not a child, but woman almost old,
Whose coal-black hair had partly turned to grey,
With sorrow and with madness; and she dwelt,
Not in that room high on the cliff, but down,
Low down within the margin of spring tides."
And then she told me all she knew of her,
As we drove onward through the sunny day.
It was a simple tale, with few, few facts;
A life that clomb one mountain and looked forth;
Then sudden sank to a low dreary plain,
And wandered ever in the sound of waves,
Till fear and fascination overcame,
And led her trembling into life and joy.
Alas! how many such are told by night,
In fisher-cottages along the shore!
   Farewell, old summer-day; I lay you by,
To tell my story, and the thoughts that rise
Within a heart that never dared believe
A life was at the mercy of a sea.
   THE STORY.
   Aye as it listeth blows the listless wind,
Filling great sails, and bending lordly masts,
Or making billows in the green corn fields,
And hunting lazy clouds across the blue:
Now, like a vapour o'er the sunny sea,
It blows the vessel from the harbour's mouth,
Out 'mid the broken crests of seaward waves,
And hovering of long-pinioned ocean birds,
As if the white wave-spots had taken wing.
But though all space is full of spots of white,
The sailor sees the little handkerchief
That flutters still, though wet with heavy tears

Which draw it earthward from the sunny wind.
Blow, wind! draw out the cord that binds the twain,
And breaks not, though outlengthened till the maid
Can only say, *I know he is not here.*
Blow, wind! yet gently; gently blow, O wind!
And let love's vision slowly, gently die;
And the dim sails pass ghost-like o'er the deep,
Lingering a little o'er the vanished hull,
With a white farewell to the straining eyes.
For never more in morning's level beam,
Will the wide wings of her sea-shadowing sails
From the green-billowed east come dancing in;
Nor ever, gliding home beneath the stars,
With a faint darkness o'er the fainter sea,
Will she, the ocean-swimmer, send a cry
Of home-come sailors, that shall wake the streets
With sudden pantings of dream-scaring joy.
Blow gently, wind! blow slowly, gentle wind!
   Weep not, oh maiden! tis not time to weep;
Torment not thou thyself before thy time;
The hour will come when thou wilt need thy tears
To cool the burning of thy desert brain.
Go to thy work; break into song sometimes,
To die away forgotten in the lapse
Of dreamy thought, ere natural pause ensue;
Oft in the day thy time-outspeeding heart,
Sending thy ready eye to scout the east,
Like child that wearies of her mother's pace,
And runs before, and yet perforce must wait.
   The time drew nigh. Oft turning from her work,
With bare arms and uncovered head she clomb
The landward slope of the prophetic hill;
From whose green head, as on the verge of time,
Seer-like she gazed, shading her hope-rapt eyes
From the bewilderment of work-day light,
Far out on the eternity of waves;
If from the Hades of the nether world
Her prayers might draw the climbing skyey sails
Up o'er the threshold of the horizon line;
For when he came she was to be his wife,
And celebrate with rites of church and home
The apotheosis of maidenhood.
   Time passed. The shadow of a fear that hung
Far off upon the horizon of her soul,
Drew near with deepening gloom and clearing form,
Till it o'erspread and filled her atmosphere,

And lost all shape, because it filled all space,
Reaching beyond the bounds of consciousness;
But ever in swift incarnations darting
Forth from its infinite a stony stare,
A blank abyss, an awful emptiness.
Ah, God! why are our souls, lone helpless seas,
Tortured with such immitigable storm?
What is this love, that now on angel wing
Sweeps us amid the stars in passionate calm;
And now with demon arms fast cincturing,
Drops us, through all gyrations of keen pain,
Down the black vortex, till the giddy whirl
Gives fainting respite to the ghastly brain?
Not these the maiden's questions. Comes he yet?
Or am I widowed ere my wedding day?
 Ah! ranged along our shores, on peak or cliff,
Or stone-ribbed promontory, or pier head,
Maidens have aye been standing; the same pain
Deadening the heart-throb; the same gathering mist
Dimming the eye that would be keen as death;
The same fixed longing on the changeless face.
Over the edge he vanished—came no more:
There, as in childhood's dreams, upon that line,
Without a parapet to shield the sense,
Voidness went sheer down to oblivion:
Over that edge he vanished—came no more.
 O happy those for whom the Possible
Opens its gates of madness, and becomes
The Real around them! those to whom henceforth
There is but one to-morrow, the next morn,
Their wedding day, ever one step removed;
The husband's foot ever upon the verge
Of the day's threshold; whiteness aye, and flowers,
Ready to meet him, ever in a dream!
But faith and expectation conquer still;
And so her morrow comes at last, and leads
The death-pale maiden-ghost, dazzled, confused,
Into the land whose shadows fall on ours,
And are our dreams of too deep blessedness.
May not some madness be a kind of faith?
Shall not the Possible become the Real?
Lives not the God who hath created dreams?
So stand we questioning upon the shore,
And gazing hopeful towards the Unrevealed.
 Long looked the maiden, till the visible
Half vanished from her eyes; the earth had ceased

That lay behind her, and the sea was all;
Except the narrow shore, which yet gave room
For her sea-haunting feet; where solid land,
Where rocks and hills stopped, frighted, suddenly,
And earth flowed henceforth on in trembling waves,
A featureless, a half re-molten world,
Halfway to the Unseen; the Invisible
Half seen in the condensed and flowing sky
Which lay so grimly smooth before her eyes
And brain and shrinking soul; where power of man
Could never heap up moles or pyramids,
Or dig a valley in the unstable gulf
Fighting for aye to make invisible,
To swallow up, and keep her smooth blue smile
Unwrinkled and unspotted with the land;
Not all the changes on the restless wave,
Saving it from a still monotony,
Whose only utterance was a dreary song
Of stifled wailing on the shrinking shore.
   Such frenzy slow invaded the poor girl.
Not hers the hovering sense of marriage bells
Tuning the air with fragrance of sweet sound;
But the low dirge that ever rose and died,
Recurring without pause or any close,
Like one verse chaunted aye in sleepless brain.
Down to the shore it drew her from the heights,
Like witch's demon-spell, that fearful moan.
She knew that somewhere in the green abyss
His body swung in curves of watery force,
Now in a circle slow revolved, and now
Swaying like wind-swung bell, when surface waves
Sank their roots deep enough to reach the waif,
Hither and thither, idly to and fro,
Wandering unheeding through the heedless sea.
A kind of fascination seized her brain,
And drew her onward to the ridgy rocks
That ran a little way into the deep,
Like questions asked of Fate by longing hearts,
Bound which the eternal ocean breaks in sighs.
Along their flats, and furrows, and jagged backs,
Out to the lonely point where the green mass
Arose and sank, heaved slow and forceful, she
Went; and recoiled in terror; ever drawn,
Ever repelled, with inward shuddering
At the great, heartless, miserable depth.
She thought the ocean lay in wait for her,

Enticing her with horror's glittering eye,
And with the hope that in an hour sure fixed
In some far century, aeons remote,
She, conscious still of love, despite the sea,
Should, in the washing of perennial waves,
Sweep o'er some stray bone, or transformed dust
Of him who loved her on this happy earth,
Known by a dreamy thrill in thawing nerves.
For so the fragments of wild songs she sung
Betokened, as she sat and watched the tide,
Till, as it slowly grew, it touched her feet;
When terror overcame—she rose and fled
Towards the shore with fear-bewildered eye;
And, stumbling on the rocks with hasty steps,
Cried, "They are coming, coming at my heels."
  Perhaps like this the songs she used to wail
In the rough northern tongue of Aberdeen:—
    Ye'll hae me yet, ye'll hae me yet,
      Sae lang an' braid, an' never a hame!
    Its nae the depth I fear a bit,
      But oh, the wideness, aye the same!
    The jaws[1] come up, wi' eerie bark;
      Cryin' I'm creepy, cauld, an' green;
    Come doon, come doon, he's lyin' stark,
      Come doon an' steek his glowerin' een.
    Syne wisht! they haud their weary roar,
      An' slide awa', an' I grow sleepy:
    Or lang, they're up aboot my door,
      Yowlin', I'm cauld, an' weet, an' creepy!
    O dool, dool! ye are like the tide—
      Ye mak' a feint awa' to gang;
    But lang awa' ye winna bide,—
      An' better greet than aye think lang.
  [Footnote 1: Jaws: *English*, breakers.]
  Where'er she fled, the same voice followed her;
Whisperings innumerable of water-drops
Growing together to a giant voice;
That sometimes in hoarse, rushing undertones,
Sometimes in thunderous peals of billowy shouts,
Called after her to come, and make no stay.
From the dim mists that brooded seaward far,
And from the lonely tossings of the waves,
Where rose and fell the raving wilderness,
Voices, pursuing arms, and beckoning hands,
Reached shorewards from the shuddering mystery.
Then sometimes uplift, on a rocky peak,

A lonely form betwixt the sea and sky,
Watchers on shore beheld her fling wild arms
High o'er her head in tossings like the waves;
Then fix them, with clasped hands of prayer intense,
Forward, appealing to the bitter sea.
Then sudden from her shoulders she would tear
Her garments, one by one, and cast them far
Into the roarings of the heedless surge,
A vain oblation to the hungry waves.
Such she did mean it; and her pitying friends
Clothed her in vain—their gifts did bribe the sea.
But such a fire was burning in her brain,
The cold wind lapped her, and the sleet-like spray
Flashed, all unheeded, on her tawny skin.
As oft she brought her food and flung it far,
Reserving scarce a morsel for her need—
Flung it—with naked arms, and streaming hair
Floating like sea-weed on the tide of wind,
Coal-black and lustreless—to feed the sea.
But after each poor sacrifice, despair,
Like the returning wave that bore it far,
Rushed surging back upon her sickening heart;
While evermore she moaned, low-voiced, between—
Half-muttered and half-moaned: "Ye'll hae me yet;
Ye'll ne'er be saired, till ye hae ta'en mysel'."
   And as the night grew thick upon the sea,
Quenching it all, except its voice of storm;
Blotting it from the region of the eye,
Though still it tossed within the haunted brain,
Entering by the portals of the ears,—
She step by step withdrew; like dreaming man,
Who, power of motion all but paralysed,
With an eternity of slowness, drags
His earth-bound, lead-like, irresponsive feet
Back from a living corpse's staring eyes;
Till on the narrow beach she turned her round.
Then, clothed in all the might of the Unseen,
Terror grew ghostly; and she shrieked and fled
Up to the battered base of the old tower,
And round the rock, and through the arched gap,
Cleaving the blackness of the vault within;
Then sank upon the sand, and gasped, and raved.
This was her secret chamber, this her place
Of refuge from the outstretched demon-deep,
All eye and voice for her, Argus more dread
Than he with hundred lidless watching orbs.

There, cowering in a nook, she sat all night,
Her eyes fixed on the entrance of the cave,
Through which a pale light shimmered from the sea,
Until she slept, and saw the sea in dreams.
Except in stormy nights, when all was dark,
And the wild tempest swept with slanting wing
Against her refuge; and the heavy spray
Shot through the doorway serpentine cold arms
To seize the fore-doomed morsel of the sea:
Then she slept never; and she would have died,
But that she evermore was stung to life
By new sea-terrors. Sometimes the sea-gull
With clanging pinions darted through the arch,
And flapped them round her face; sometimes a wave,
If tides were high and winds from off the sea,
Rushed through the door, and in its watery mesh
Clasped her waist-high, then out again to sea!
Out to the devilish laughter and the fog!
While she clung screaming to the bare rock-wall;
Then sat unmoving, till the low grey dawn
Grew on the misty dance of spouting waves,
That mixed the grey with white; picture one-hued,
Seen in the framework of the arched door:
Then the old fascination drew her out,
Till, wrapt in misty spray, moveless she stood
Upon the border of the dawning sea.
   And yet she had a chamber in her soul,
The innermost of all, a quiet place;
But which she could not enter for the love
That kept her out for ever in the storm.
Could she have entered, all had been as still
As summer evening, or a mother's arms;
And she had found her lost love sleeping there.
Thou too hast such a chamber, quiet place,
Where God is waiting for thee. Is it gain,
Or the confused murmur of the sea
Of human voices on the rocks of fame,
That will not let thee enter? Is it care
For the provision of the unborn day,
As if thou wert a God that must foresee,
Lest his great sun should chance forget to rise?
Or pride that thou art some one in the world,
And men must bow before thee? Oh! go mad
For love of some one lost; for some old voice
Which first thou madest sing, and after sob;
Some heart thou foundest rich, and leftest bare,

Choking its well of faith with thy false deeds;
Not like thy God, who keeps the better wine
Until the last, and, if He giveth grief,
Giveth it first, and ends the tale with joy.
Madness is nearer God than thou: go mad,
And be ennobled far above thyself.
Her brain was ill, her heart was well: she loved.
It was the unbroken cord between the twain
That drew her ever to the ocean marge;
Though to her feverous phantasy, unfit,
'Mid the tumultuous brood of shapes distort,
To see one simple form, it was the fear
Of fixed destiny, unavoidable,
And not the longing for the well-known face,
That drew her, drew her to the urgent sea.
Better to die, better to rave for love,
Than to recover with sick sneering heart.
  Or, if that thou art noble, in some hour,
Maddened with thoughts of that which could not be,
Thou mightst have yielded to the burning wind,
That swept in tempest through thy scorching brain,
And rushed into the thick cold night of the earth,
And clamoured to the waves and beat the rocks;
And never found the way back to the seat
Of conscious rule, and power to bear thy pain;
But God had made thee stronger to endure
For other ends, beyond thy present choice:
Wilt thou not own her story a fit theme
For poet's tale? in her most frantic mood,
Not call the maniac *sister*, tenderly?
For she went mad for love and not for gold.
And in the faded form, whose eyes, like suns
Too fierce for freshness and for dewy bloom,
Have parched and paled the hues of tender spring,
Cannot thy love unmask a youthful shape
Deformed by tempests of the soul and sea,
Fit to remind thee of a story old
Which God has in his keeping—of thyself?
  But God forgets not men because they sleep.
The darkness lasts all night and clears the eyes;
Then comes the morning and the joy of light.
O surely madness hideth not from Him;
Nor doth a soul cease to be beautiful
In His sight, when its beauty is withdrawn,
And hid by pale eclipse from human eyes.
Surely as snow is friendly to the spring,

A madness may be friendly to the soul,
And shield it from a more enduring loss,
From the ice-spears of a heart-reaching frost.
So, after years, the winter of her life,
Came the sure spring to her men had forgot,
Closing the rent links of the social chain,
And leaving her outside their charmed ring.
Into the chill wind and the howling night,
God sent out for her, and she entered in
Where there was no more sea. What messengers
Ran from the door of love-contented heaven,
To lead her towards the real ideal home?
The sea, her terror, and the wintry wind.
For, on a morn of sunshine, while the wind
Yet blew, and heaved yet the billowy sea
With memories of the night of deep unrest,
They found her in a basin of the rocks,
Which, buried in a firmament of sea
When ocean winds heap up the tidal waves,
Yet, in the respiration of the surge,
Lifts clear its edge of rock, full to the brim
With deep, clear, resting water, plentiful.
There, in the blessedness of sleep, which God
Gives his beloved, she lay drowned and still.
O life of love, conquered at last by fate!
O life raised from the dead by Saviour Death!
O love unconquered and invincible!
The sea had cooled the burning of that brain;
Had laid to rest those limbs so fever-tense,
That scarce relaxed in sleep; and now she lies
Sleeping the sleep that follows after pain.
'Twas one night more of agony and fear,
Of shrinking from the onset of the sea;
One cry of desolation, when her fear
Became a fact, and then,—God knows the rest.
O cure of all our miseries—*God knows!*

   O thou whose feet tread ever the wet sands
And howling rocks along the wearing shore,
Roaming the confines of the endless sea!
Strain not thine eyes across, bedimmed with tears;
No sail comes back across that tender line.
Turn thee unto thy work, let God alone;
He will do his part. Then across the waves
Will float faint whispers from the better land,
Veiled in the dust of waters we call storms,

To thine averted ears. Do thou thy work,
And thou shalt follow; follow, and find thine own.
   O thou who liv'st in fear of the *To come!*
Around whose house the storm of terror breaks
All night; to whose love-sharpened ear, all day,
The Invisible is calling at thy door,
To render up that which thou can'st not keep,
Be it a life or love! Open thy door,
And carry forth thy dead unto the marge
Of the great sea; bear it into the flood,
Braving the cold that creepeth to thy heart,
And lay thy coffin as an ark of hope
Upon the billows of the infinite sea.
Give God thy dead to keep: so float it back,
With sighs and prayers to waft it through the dark,
Back to the spring of life. Say—"It is dead,
But thou, the life of life, art yet alive,
And thou can'st give the dead its dear old life,
With new abundance perfecting the old.
God, see my sadness; feel it in thyself."
   Ah God! the earth is full of cries and moans,
And dull despair, that neither moans nor cries;
Thousands of hearts are waiting the last day,
For what they know not, but with hope of change,
Of resurrection, or of dreamless death.
Raise thou the buried dead of springs gone by
In maidens' bosoms; raise the autumn fruits
Of old men feebly mournful o'er the life
Which scarce hath memory but the mournfulness.
There is no Past with thee: bring back once more
The summer eves of lovers, over which
The wintry wind that raveth through the world
Heaps wretched leaves, half tombed in ghastly snow;
Bring back the mother-heaven of orphans lone,
The brother's and the sister's faithfulness;
Bring forth the kingdom of the Son of Man.
   They troop around me, children wildly crying;
Women with faded eyes, all spent of tears;
Men who have lived for love, yet lived alone;
And worse than so, whose grief cannot be said.
O God, thou hast a work to do indeed
To save these hearts of thine with full content,
Except thou give them Lethe's stream to drink,
And that, my God, were all unworthy thee.
   Dome up, O Heaven! yet higher o'er my head;
Back, back, horizon! widen out my world;

Rush in, O infinite sea of the Unknown!
For, though he slay me, I will trust in God.

MY HEART.

I heard, in darkness, on my bed,
  The beating of my heart
To servant feet and regnant head
  A common life impart,
By the liquid cords, in every thread
  Unbroken as they start.

  Night, with its power to silence day,
  Filled up my lonely room;
All motion quenching, save what lay
  Beyond its passing doom,
Where in his shed the workman gay
  Went on despite the gloom.

  I listened, and I knew the sound,
  And the trade that he was plying;
For backwards, forwards, bound and bound,
  'Twas a shuttle, flying, flying;
Weaving ever life's garment round,
  Till the weft go out with sighing.

  I said, O mystic thing, thou goest
  On working in the dark;
In space's shoreless sea thou rowest,
  Concealed within thy bark;
All wondrous things thou, wonder, showest,
  Yet dost not any mark.

  For all the world is woven by thee,
  Besides this fleshly dress;
With earth and sky thou clothest me,
  Form, distance, loftiness;
A globe of glory spouting free
  Around the visionless.

  For when thy busy efforts fail,
  And thy shuttle moveless lies,
They will fall from me, like a veil
  From before a lady's eyes;
As a night-perused, just-finished tale
  In the new daylight dies.

  But not alone dost thou unroll
  The mountains, fields, and seas,
A mighty, wonder-painted scroll,
  Like the Patmos mysteries;
Thou mediator 'twixt my soul
  And higher things than these.

In holy ephod clothing me
Thou makest me a seer;
In all the lovely things I see,
The inner truths appear;
And the deaf spirit without thee
No spirit-word could hear.
Yet though so high thy mission is,
And thought to spirit brings,
Thy web is but the chrysalis,
Where lie the future wings,
Now growing into perfectness
By thy inwoven things.
Then thou, God's pulse, wilt cease to beat;
But His heart will still beat on,
Weaving another garment meet,
If needful for his son;
And sights more glorious, to complete
The web thou hast begun.

O DO NOT LEAVE ME.

O do not leave me, mother, till I sleep;
Be near me until I forget; sit there.
And the child having prayed lest she should weep,
Sleeps in the strength of prayer.
O do not leave me, lover, brother, friends,
Till I am dead, and resting in my place.
And the girl, having prayed, in silence bends
Down to the earth's embrace.
Leave me not, God, until—nay, until when?
Not till I have with thee one heart, one mind;
Not till the Life is Light in me, and then
Leaving is left behind.

THE HOLY SNOWDROPS.

Of old, with goodwill from the skies,
The holy angels came;
They walked the earth with human eyes,
And passed away in flame.
But now the angels are withdrawn,
Because the flowers can speak;
With Christ, we see the dayspring dawn
In every snowdrop meek.
God sends them forth; to God they tend;
Not less with love they burn,
That to the earth they lowly bend,
And unto dust return.
No miracle in them hath place,
For this world is their home;

An utterance of essential grace
  The angel-snowdrops come.
TO MY SISTER.
  O sister, God is very good—
  Thou art a woman now:
O sister, be thy womanhood
  A baptism on thy brow!
    For what?—Do ancient stories lie
    Of Titans long ago,
The children of the lofty sky
  And mother earth below?
    Nay, walk not now upon the ground
    Some sons of heavenly mould?
Some daughters of the Holy, found
  In earthly garments' fold?
    He said, who did and spoke the truth:
    "Gods are the sons of God."
And so the world's Titanic youth
  Strives homeward by one road.
    Then live thou, sister, day and night,
    An earth-child of the sky,
For ever climbing up the height
  Of thy divinity.
    Still in thy mother's heart-embrace,
    Waiting thy hour of birth,
Thou growest by the genial grace
  Of the child-bearing earth.
    Through griefs and joys, each sad and sweet,
    Thou shalt attain the end;
Till then a goddess incomplete—
  O evermore my friend!
    Nor is it pride that striveth so:
    The height of the Divine
Is to be lowly 'mid the low;
  No towering cloud—a mine;
    A mine of wealth and warmth and song,
    An ever-open door;
For when divinely born ere long,
  A woman thou the more.
    For at the heart of womanhood
    The child's great heart doth lie;
At childhood's heart, the germ of good,
  Lies God's simplicity.
    So, sister, be thy womanhood
    A baptism on thy brow

For something dimly understood,
  And which thou art not now;
  But which within thee, all the time,
  Maketh thee what thou art;
Maketh thee long and strive and climb—
  The God-life at thy heart.

OH THOU OF LITTLE FAITH!
  Sad-hearted, be at peace: the snowdrop lies
  Under the cold, sad earth-clods and the snow;
But spring is floating up the southern skies,
  And the pale snowdrop silent waits below.
  O loved if known! in dull December's day
  One scarce believes there is a month of June;
But up the stairs of April and of May
  The dear sun climbeth to the summer's noon.
  Dear mourner! I love God, and so I rest;
  O better! God loves thee, and so rest thou:
He is our spring-time, our dim-visioned Best,
  And He will help thee—do not fear the *How.*

LONGING.
  My heart is full of inarticulate pain,
  And beats laboriously. Ungenial looks
Invade my sanctuary. Men of gain,
  Wise in success, well-read in feeble books,
Do not come near me now, your air is drear;
'Tis winter and low skies when ye appear.
  Beloved, who love beauty and love truth!
  Come round me; for too near ye cannot come;
Make me an atmosphere with your sweet youth;
  Give me your souls to breathe in, a large room;
Speak not a word, for see, my spirit lies
Helpless and dumb; shine on me with your eyes.
  O all wide places, far from feverous towns!
  Great shining seas! pine forests! mountains wild!
Rock-bosomed shores! rough heaths! and sheep-cropt downs!
  Vast pallid clouds! blue spaces undefiled!
Room! give me room! give loneliness and air!
  Free things and plenteous in your regions fair.
  White dove of David, flying overhead,
  Golden with sunlight on thy snowy wings,
Outspeeding thee my longing thoughts have fled
  To find a home afar from men and things;
Where in his temple, earth o'erarched with sky,
God's heart to mine may speak, my heart reply.
  O God of mountains, stars, and boundless spaces!
  O God of freedom and of joyous hearts!

When thy face looketh forth from all men's faces,
  There will be room enough in crowded marts;
Brood thou around me, and the noise is o'er;
Thy universe my closet with shut door.
    Heart, heart, awake! the love that loveth all
    Maketh a deeper calm than Horeb's cave.
God in thee, can his children's folly gall?
    Love may be hurt, but shall not love be brave?—
Thy holy silence sinks in dews of balm;
Thou art my solitude, my mountain-calm.

A BOY'S GRIEF.

Ah me! in ages far away,
  The good, the heavenly land,
Though unbeheld, quite near them lay,
  And men could understand.
    The dead yet find it, who, when here,
    Did love it more than this;
They enter in, are filled with cheer,
  And pain expires in bliss.
    Oh, fairly shines the blessed land!
    Ah, God! I weep and pray—
The heart thou holdest in thy hand
  Loves more this sunny day.
    I see the hundred thousand wait
    Around the radiant throne:
To me it is a dreary state,
  A crowd of beings lone.
    I do not care for singing psalms;
    I tire of good men's talk;
To me there is no joy in palms,
  Or white-robed solemn walk.
    I love to hear the wild winds meet,
    The wild old winds at night;
To watch the starlight throb and beat,
  To wait the thunder-light.
    I love all tales of valiant men,
    Of women good and fair;
If I were rich and strong, ah then,
  I would do something rare.
    I see thy temple in the skies
    On pillars strong and white;
I cannot love it, though I rise
  And try with all my might.
    Sometimes a joy lays hold on me,
    And I am speechless then;

Almost a martyr I could be,
  And join the holy men.
  But soon my heart is like a clod,
  My spirit wrapt in doubt—
"*A pillar in the house of God,*
  And never more go out!"
  No more the sunny, breezy morn;
  No more the speechless moon;
No more the ancient hills, forlorn,
  A vision, and a boon.
  Ah, God! my love will never burn,
  Nor shall I taste thy joy;
And Jesus' face is calm and stern—
  I am a hapless boy.

THE CHILD-MOTHER.

  Heavily lay the warm sunlight
Upon the green blades shining bright,
  An outspread grassy sea:
She through the burnished yellow flowers
Went walking in the golden hours
  That slept upon the lea.

  The bee went past her with a hum;
The merry gnats did go and come
  In complicated dance;
Like a blue angel, to and fro,
The splendid dragon-fly did go,
  Shot like a seeking glance.

  She never followed them, but still
Went forward with a quiet will,
  That got, but did not miss;
With gentle step she passed along,
And once a low, half-murmured song
  Uttered her share of bliss.

  It was a little maiden-child;
You see, not frolicsome and wild,
  As such a child should be;
For though she was just nine, no more,
Another little child she bore,
  Almost as big as she.

  With tender care of straining arms,
She kept it circled from all harms,
  With face turned from the sun;
For in that perfect tiny heart,
The mother, sister, nurse, had part,
  Her womanhood begun.

At length they reach an ugly ditch,
The slippery sloping bank of which
　Flowers and long grasses line;
Some ragged-robins baby spied,
And spread his little arms out wide,
　As he had found a mine.
　What baby wants, that baby has:
A law unalterable as—
　The poor shall serve the rich;
She kneeleth down with eager eyes,
And, reaching far out for the prize,
　Topples into the ditch.
　And slanting down the bank she rolled,
But in her little bosom's fold
　She clasps the baby tight;
And in the ditch's muddy flow,
No safety sought by letting go,
　At length she stands upright.
　Alas! her little feet are wet;
Her new shoes! how can she forget?
　And yet she does not cry.
Her scanty frock of dingy blue,
Her petticoat wet through and through!
　But baby is quite dry.
　And baby laughs, and baby crows;
And baby being right, she knows
　That nothing can be wrong;
And so with troubled heart, yet stout,
She plans how ever to get out,
　With meditations long.
　The bank is higher than her head,
And slippery too, as I have said;
　And what to do with baby?
For even the monkey, when he goes,
Needs both his fingers and his toes.—
　She is perplexed as may be.
　But all her puzzling was no good,
Though staring up the bank she stood,
　Which, as she sunk, grew higher;
Until, invaded with dismay,
Lest baby's patience should give way,
　She frees her from the mire.
　And up and down the ditch, not glad,
But patient, she did promenade;
　Splash! splash! went her poor feet.
And baby thought it rare good fun,

And did not want it to be done;
  And the ditch flowers were sweet.
  But, oh! the world that she had left,
The meads from her so lately reft,
  An infant Proserpine,
Lay like a fabled land above,
A paradise of sunny love,
  In warmth and light divine.
  While, with the hot sun overhead,
She her low watery way did tread,
  'Mid slimy weeds and frogs;
While now and then from distant field
The sound of laughter faintly pealed,
  Or bark of village dogs.
  And once the ground began to shake,
And her poor little heart to quake
  For fear of added woes;
Till, looking up, at last, perforce,
She saw the head of a huge horse
  Go past upon its nose.
  And with a sound of tearing grass,
And puffing breath that awful was,
  And horns of frightful size,
A cow looked through the broken hedge,
And gazed down on her from the edge,
  With great big Juno eyes.
  And so the sun went on and on,
And horse and cow and horns were gone,
  And still no help came near;
Till at the last she heard the sound
Of human footsteps on the ground,
  And then she cried: "*I'm here!*"
  It was a man, much to her joy,
Who looked amazed at girl and boy,
  And reached his hand so strong.
"Give me the child," he said; but no,
She would not let the baby go,
  She had endured too long.
  So, with a smile at her alarms,
He stretched down both his lusty arms,
  And lifted them together;
And, having thanked her helper, she
Did hasten homeward painfully,
  Wet in the sunny weather.
  At home at length, lo! scarce a speck
Was on the child from heel to neck,

Though she was sorely mired;
Nor gave she sign of grief's unrest,
Till, hid upon her mother's breast,
  She wept till she was tired.
  And intermixed with sobbing wail,
She told her mother all the tale,—
  "But"—here her wet cheeks glow—
"Mother, I did not, through it all,
I did not once let baby fall—
  I never let him go."
  Ah me! if on this star-world's face
We men and women had like grace
  To bear and shield each other;
Our race would soon be young again,
Its heart as free of ache and pain
  As that of this child-mother.

LOVE'S ORDEAL;
A recollection and attempted completion of a prose fragment read in childhood.

"Know'st thou that sound upon the window pane?"
Said the youth quietly, as outstretched he lay,
Where for an hour outstretched he had lain,
Pillowed upon her knees. To him did say
The thoughtful maiden: "It is but the rain
That hath been gathering in the West all day;
Be still, my dearest, let my eyes yet rest
Awhile upon thy face so calm and blest."
  "Know'st thou that sound, from silence slowly wrought?"
Said the youth, and his eyelids softly rose,
Revealing to her eyes the depths of thought
That lay beneath her in a still repose.
"I know it," said the maiden; "it is nought
But the loud wintry wind that ever blows,
Swinging the great arms of the dreary pines,
Which each with others in its pain entwines."
  "Hear'st thou the baying of my hounds?" said he;
"Draw back the lattice-bar and let them in."
Through a cloud-rift the light fell noiselessly
Upon the cottage floor; and, gaunt and thin,
Leaped in the stag-hounds, bounding as in glee,
Shaking the rain-drops from their shaggy skin;
And as the maiden closed the spattered glass,
A shadow faint over the floor did pass.
  The youth, half-raised, was leaning on his hand;
And when again beside him sat the maid,
His eyes for a slow minute moving scanned

Her calm peace-lighted face; and then he said,
Monotonous, like solemn-read command:
"For love is of the earth, earthy, and laid
Down lifeless in its mother's womb at last."
The strange sound through the great pine-branches passed.
   Again a shadow as it were of glass,
Over the moonbeams on the cottage floor,
Shapeless and dim, almost unseen, doth pass;
A mingled sound of rain-drops at the door,
But not a sound upon the window was.
A look of sorrowing doubt the youth's face wore;
And the two hounds half-rose, and gazed at him,
Eyeing his countenance by the taper dim.
   Now nothing of these things the maiden noted,
But turned her face with half-reproachful look,
As doubting whether he the words had quoted
Out of some evil, earth-begotten book;
Or upward from his spirit's depths had floated
Those words like bubbles in a low dead brook;
But his eyes seemed to question,—Yea or No;
And so the maiden answered: "'Tis not so;
   "Love is of heaven, and heavenly." A faint smile
Parted his lips, as a thought unexpressed
Were speaking in his heart; and for a while
He gently laid his head upon her breast;
His thought, a bark that by a sunny isle
At length hath found the haven of its rest,
Yet must not long remain, but forward go:
He lifted up his head, and answered: "No—
   "Maiden, I have loved other maidens." Pale
Her red lips grew. "I loved them; yes, but they,
One after one, in trial's hour did fail;
For after sunset, clouds again are grey."
A sudden light flashed through the silken veil
That drooping hid her eyes; and then there lay
A stillness on her face, waiting; and then
The little clock rung out the hour of ten.
   Moaning again the great pine-branches bow,
As if they tried in vain the wind to stem.
Still looking in her eyes, the youth said—"Thou
Art not more beautiful than some of them;
But more of earnestness is on thy brow;
Thine eyes are beaming like some dark-bright gem
That pours from hidden heart upon the night
The rays it gathered from the noon-day light.

"Look on this hand, beloved; thou didst see
The horse that broke from many, it did hold:
Two hours shall pass away, and it will be
All withered up and dry, wrinkled and old,
Big-veined, and skinny to extremity."
Calmly upon him looked the maiden bold;
The stag-hounds rose, and gazed on him, and then,
With a low whine, laid themselves down again.
   A minute's silence, and the youth spake on:
"Dearest, I have a fearful thing to bear"
(A pain-cloud crossed his face, and then was gone)
"At midnight, when the moon sets; wilt thou dare
To go with me, or must I go alone
To meet an agony that will not spare?"
She spoke not, rose, and towards her mantle went;
His eyes did thank her—she was well content.
   "Not yet, not yet; it is not time; for see
The hands have far to travel to the hour;
Yet time is scarcely left for telling thee
The past and present, and the coming power
Of the great darkness that will fall on me:
Roses and jasmine twine the bridal bower—
If ever bower and bridal joy be mine,
Horror and darkness must that bower entwine."
   Under his head the maiden put her arm,
And knelt beside, half leaning on his breast;
As, soul and body, she would shield all harm
From him whose love had made her being blest;
And well the healing of her eyes might charm
His doubting thoughts again to trusting rest.
He drew and hid her face his heart upon,
Then spoke with low voice sounding changeless on.
   Strange words they were, and fearful, that he spake;
The maiden moved not once, nor once replied;
And ever as he spoke, the wind did make
A feebler moan until away it died;
Then the rain ceased, and not a movement brake
The silence, save the clock that did divide
The hours into quick moments, sparks of time
Scorching the soul that watcheth for the chime.
   He spoke of sins that pride had caused in him;
Of sufferings merciful, and wanderings wild;
Of fainting noontides, and of oceans dim;
Of earthly beauty that had oft beguiled;
And then the sudden storm and contest grim;
From each emerging new-born, more a child;

Wandering again throughout the teaching earth,
No rest attaining, only a new birth.
   "But when I find a heart that's like to mine,
With love to live through the unloving hour,
Folded in faith, like violets that have lien
Folded in warm earth, till the sunny shower
Calleth them forth; thoughts with my thoughts to twine,
Weaving around us both a fragrant bower,
Where we within may sleep, together drawn,
Folded in love until the morning dawn;
   "Then shall I rest, my weary day's work o'er,
A deep sleep bathing, steeping all my soul,
Dissolving out the earth-stains evermore.
Thou too shalt sleep with me, and be made whole.
All, all time's billows over us shall pour,
Then ebb away, and far beneath us roll:
We shall behold them like a stormy lake,
'Neath the clear height of peace where we awake."
   Her face on his, her lips on his lips pressed,
Was the sole answer that the maiden made.
With both his arms he held her to his breast;
'Twas but a moment; yet, before he said
One other word, of power to strengthen, lest
She should give way amid the trial dread,
The clock gave out the warning to the hour,
And on the thatch fell sounds as of a shower.
   One long kiss, and the maiden rose. A fear
Fell like a shadow dim upon her heart,
A trembling as at something ghostly near;
But she was bold, for they were not to part.
Then the youth rose, his cheek pale, his eyes clear;
And helped the maid, whose trembling hands did thwart
Her haste to tie her gathered mantle's fold;
Then forth they went into the midnight cold.
   The moon was sunken low in the dim west,
Curled upwards on the steep horizon's brink,
A leaf of glory falling to its rest.
The maiden's hand, still trembling, scarce could link
Her to his side; but his arm round her waist
Stole gently; so she walked, and did not sink;
Her hand on his right side soon held him fast,
And so together wound, they onward passed.
   And, clinging to his side, she felt full well
The strong and measured beating of his heart;
But as the floating moon aye lower fell,
Slowly she felt its bounding force depart,

Till like a throbbing bird; nor can she tell
Whether it beats, at length; and with a start
She felt the arm relax around her flung,
And on her circling arm he leaned and hung.
  But as his steps more and more feeble grow,
She feels her strength and courage rise amain.
He lifted up his head; the moon was low,
Almost on the world's edge. A smile of pain
Was on his lips, as his large eyes turned slow
Seeking for hers; which, like a heavy rain,
Poured love on him in many a love-lit gleam.
So they walked like two souls, linked by one dream.[2]
  [Footnote 2:
> In a lovely garden walking,
>   Two lovers went hand in hand;
> Two wan, sick figures, talking,
>   They sat in the flowery land.
> On the cheek they kissed each other,
>   And they kissed upon the mouth;
> Fast clasped they one another—
>   And back came their health and youth.
> Two little bells rang shrilly,
>   And the dream went with the hour:
> She lay in the cloister stilly,
>   He far in the dungeon-tower.

Translated from Uhland.]
Hanging his head, behind each came a hound,
With slow and noiseless paws upon the road.
What is that shining on the weedy ground?
Nought but the bright eyes of the dingy toad.
The silent pines range every way around;
A deep stream on the left side hardly flowed.
Their path is towards the moon, dying alone—
It touches the horizon, dips, is gone.
  Its last gleam fell upon dim glazed eyes;
An old man tottered feebly in her hold,
Stooping with bended knees that could not rise;
Nor longer could his arm her waist infold.
The maiden trembled; but through this disguise
Her love beheld what never could grow old;
And so the aged man, she, young and warm,
Clasped closer yet with her supporting arm.
  Till with short, dragging steps, he turned aside
Into a closer thicket of tall firs,
Whose bare, straight, slender stems behind them hide
A smooth grey rock. Not a pine-needle stirs

Till they go in. Then a low wind blows wide
O'er their cone-tops. It swells until it whirrs
Through the long stems, as if aeolian chords
For moulding mystic sounds in lack of words.
  But as they entered by a narrow cleft
Into the rock's heart, suddenly it ceased;
And the tall pines stood still as if bereft
Of a strong passion, or from pain released;
Once more they wove their strange, dark, moveless weft
O'er the dull midnight sky; and in the East
A mist arose and clomb the skyey stairs;
And like sad thoughts the bats came unawares.
  'Tis a dark chamber for the bridal night,
O poor, pale, saviour bride! A faint rush-lamp
He kindled with his shaking hands; its light
Painted a tiny halo on the damp
That filled the cavern to its unseen height,
Like a death-candle on the midnight swamp.
Within, each side the entrance, lies a hound,
With liquid light his green eyes gleaming round.
  A couch just raised above the rocky floor,
Of withered oak and beech-leaves, that the wind
Had tossed about till weary, covered o'er
With skins of bears which feathery mosses lined,
And last of lambs, with wool long, soft, and hoar,
Received the old man's bended limbs reclined.
Gently the maiden did herself unclothe,
And lay beside him, trusting, and not loath.
  Again the storm among the trees o'erhead;
The hounds pricked up their ears, their eyes flashed fire;
Seemed to the trembling maiden that a tread
Light, and yet clear, amid the wind's loud ire,
As dripping feet o'er smooth slabs hither sped,
Came often up, as with a fierce desire,
To enter, but as oft made quick retreat;
And looking forth the hounds stood on their feet.
  Then came, half querulous, a whisper old,
Feeble and hollow as from out a chest:
"Take my face on your bosom, I am cold."
Straightway she bared her bosom's white soft nest;
And then his head, her gentle hands, love-bold,
With its grey withered face against her pressed.
Ah, maiden! it was very old and chill,
But thy warm heart beneath it grew not still.
  Again the wind falls, and the rain-clouds pour,
Rushing to earth; and soon she heard the sound

Of a fierce torrent through the thick night roar;
The lamp went out as by the darkness drowned;
No more the morn will dawn, oh, never more!
Like centuries the feeble hours went round;
Dead night lay o'er her, clasping, as she lay,
Within her holy place, unburied clay.

   The hours stood still; her life sunk down so low,
That, but for wretchedness, no life she knew.
A charnel wind sung on a moaning—*No;*
Earth's centre was the grave from which it blew;
Earth's loves and beauties all passed sighing slow,
Roses and lilies, children, friends, the few;
But so transparent blanched in every part,
She saw the pale worm lying in each heart.

   And worst of all, O death of gladsome life!
A voice within awoke and cried: In sooth,
There is no need of sorrow, care, and strife;
For all that women beauty call, and truth,
Is but a glow from hearts with fancy rife,
Passing away with slowly fading youth.
Gaze on them narrowly, they waver, blot;
Look at them fixedly, and they are not.

   And all the answer the poor child could make
Lay in the tightened grasp of her two hands;
She felt as if she lay mouldering awake
Within the sepulchre's fast stony bands,
And cared not though she died, but for his sake.
And the dark horror grew like drifting sands,
Till nought seemed beautiful, not God, nor light;
And yet she braved the false, denying night.

   But after hope was dead, a faint, light streak
Crept through a crevice in the rocky wall;
It fell upon her bosom and his cheek.
From God's own eye that light-glance seemed to fall.
Backward he drew his head, and did not speak,
But gazed with large deep eyes angelical
Upon her face. Old age had fled away—
Youth everlasting in her bosom lay.

   With a low cry of joy closer she crept,
And on his bosom hid a face that glowed,
Seeking amends for terror while he slept.
She had been faithful: the beloved owed
Love, youth, and gladness unto her who wept
Gushingly on his heart. Her warm tears flowed
A baptism for the life that would not cease;
And when the sun arose, they slept in peace.

A PRAYER FOR THE PAST.

All sights and sounds of every year,
All groups and forms, each leaf and gem,
Are thine, O God, nor need I fear
To speak to Thee of them.

Too great thy heart is to despise;
Thy day girds centuries about;
From things which we count small, thine eyes
See great things looking out.

Therefore this prayerful song I sing
May come to Thee in ordered words;
Therefore its sweet sounds need not cling
In terror to their chords.
* * * * *

I know that nothing made is lost;
That not a moon hath ever shone,
That not a cloud my eyes hath crost,
But to my soul hath gone.

That all the dead years garnered lie
In this gem-casket, my dim soul;
And that thy hand may, once, apply
The key that opes the whole.

But what lies dead in me, yet lives
In Thee, whose Parable is—Time,
And Worlds, and Forms, and Sound that gives
Words and the music-chime.

And after my next coming birth,
The new child's prayer will rise to Thee:
To hear again the sounds of Earth,
Its sights again to see.

With child's glad eyes to see once more
The visioned glories of the gloom,
With climbing suns, and starry store,
Ceiling my little room.

O call again the moons that glide
Behind old vapours sailing slow;
Lost sights of solemn skies that slide
O'er eyelids sunken low.

Show me the tides of dawning swell,
And lift the world's dim eastern eye,
And the dark tears that all night fell
With radiance glorify.

First I would see, oh, sore bereft!
My father's house, my childhood's home;
Where the wild snow-storms raved, and left
White mounds of frozen foam.

Till, going out one dewy morn,
A man was turning up the mould;
And in our hearts the spring was born,
Crept hither through the cold.
　　And with the glad year I would go,
The troops of daisies round my feet;
Flying the kite, or, in the glow
Of arching summer heat,
　　Outstretched in fear upon the bank,
Lest gazing up on awful space,
I should fall down into the blank
From off the round world's face.
　　And let my brothers be with me
To play our old games yet again;
And all should go as lovingly
As now that we are men.
　　If over Earth the shade of Death
Passed like a cloud's wide noiseless wing,
We'd tell a secret, in low breath:
"Mind, 'tis a *dream* of Spring.
　　"And in this dream, our brother's gone
Upstairs; he heard our father call;
For one by one we go alone,
Till he has gathered all."
　　Father, in joy our knees we bow;
This earth is not a place of tombs:
We are but in the nursery now;
They in the upper rooms.
　　For are we not at home in Thee,
And all this world a visioned show;
That, knowing what *Abroad* is, we
What *Home* is, too, may know?
　　And at thy feet I sit, O Lord,
As years ago, in moonlight pale,
I sat and heard my father's word
Reading a lofty tale.
　　So in this vision I would go
Still onward through the gliding years,
Reaping great Noontide's joyous glow,
Still Eve's refreshing tears.
　　One afternoon sit pondering
In that old chair, in that old room,
Where passing pigeon's sudden wing
Flashed lightning through the gloom.
　　There, try once more with effort vain,
To mould in one perplexed things;

And find the solace yet again
Faith in the Father brings.
   Or on my horse go wandering round,
Mid desert moors and mountains high;
While storm-clouds, darkly brooding, found
In me another sky.
   For so thy Visible grew mine,
Though half its power I could not know;
And in me wrought a work divine,
Which Thou hadst ordered so;
   Filling my brain with form and word
From thy full utterance unto men;
Shapes that might ancient Truth afford,
And find it words again.
   Till Spring, in after years of youth,
Wove its dear form with every form;
Now a glad bursting into Truth,
Now a low sighing storm.
   But in this vision of the Past,
Spring-world to summer leading in,
Whose joys but not whose sorrows last,
I have left out the sin.
   I picture but development,
Green leaves unfolding to their fruits,
Expanding flowers, aspiring scent,
But not the writhing roots.
   Then follow English sunsets, o'er
A warm rich land outspread below;
A green sea from a level shore,
Bright boats that come and go.
   And one beside me in whose eyes
Old Nature found a welcome home,
A treasury of changeful skies
Beneath a changeless dome.
   But will it still be thus, O God?
And shall I always wish to see
And trace again the hilly road
By which I went to Thee?
   We bend above a joy new given,
That gives new feelings gladsome birth;
A living gift from one in heaven
To two upon the earth.
   Are no days creeping softly on
Which I should tremble to renew?
I thank thee, Lord, for what is gone—
Thine is the future too.

And are we not at home in Thee,
And all this world a visioned show;
That knowing what *Abroad* is, we
What *Home* is, too, may know?

FAR AND NEAR.

[The fact to which the following verses refer, is related by Dr. Edward Clarke in his Travels.]

Blue sunny skies above; below,
  A blue and sunny sea;
A world of blue, wherein did blow
  One soft wind steadily.

In great and solemn heaves, the mass
  Of pulsing ocean beat,
Unwrinkled as the sea of glass
  Beneath the holy feet.

With forward leaning of desire,
  The ship sped calmly on,
A pilgrim strong that would not tire,
  Nor hasten to be gone.

The mouth of the mysterious Nile,
  Full thirty leagues away,
Breathed in his ear old tales to wile
  Old Ocean as he lay.

Low on the surface of the sea
  Faint sounds like whispers glide
Of lovers talking tremulously,
  Close by the vessel's side.

Or as within a sleeping wood
  A windy sigh awoke,
And fluttering all the leafy brood,
  The summer-silence broke.

A wayward phantasy might say
  That little ocean-maids
Were clapping little hands of play,
  Deep down in ocean-glades.

The traveller by land and flood,
  The man of ready mind,
Much questioning the reason, stood—
  No answer could he find.

That day, on Egypt's distant land,
  And far from off the shore,
Two nations fought with armed hand,
  With bellowing cannon's roar.

That fluttering whisper, low and near,
  Was the far battle-blare;

An airy rippling motion here,
  The blasting thunder there.
  And so this aching in my breast,
  Dim, faint, and undefined,
May be the sound of far unrest,
  Borne on the spirit's wind;
  The uproar of the battle fought
 Betwixt the bond and free;
The thundering roll in whispers brought
  From Heaven's artillery.

MY ROOM.
  To G.E.M.
  'Tis a little room, my friend;
A baby-walk from end to end;
All the things look sadly real,
This hot noontide's Unideal.
Seek not refuge at the casement,
There's no pasture for amazement
But a house most dim and rusty,
And a street most dry and dusty;
Seldom here more happy vision
Than water-cart's blest apparition,
We'll shut out the staring space,
Draw the curtains in its face.
  Close the eyelids of the room,
Fill it with a scarlet gloom:
Lo! the walls on every side
Are transformed and glorified;
Ceiled as with a rosy cloud
Furthest eastward of the crowd,
Blushing faintly at the bliss
Of the Titan's good-night kiss,
Which her westward sisters share,—
Crimson they from breast to hair.
'Tis the faintest lends its dye
To my room—ah, not the sky!
Worthy though to be a room
Underneath the wonder-dome:
Look around on either hand,
Are we not in fairy-land?
In the ruddy atmosphere
All familiar things appear
Glowing with a mystery
In the red light shadowy;
Lasting bliss to you and me,
Colour only though it be.

Now on the couch, inwrapt in mist
Of vapourized amethyst,
Lie, as in a rose's heart;
Secret things I will impart;
Any time you would receive them;
Easier though you will believe them
In dissolving dreamy red,
Self-same radiance that is shed
From the summer-heart of Poet,
Flushing those that never know it.
Tell me not the light thou viewest
Is a false one; 'tis the truest;
'Tis the light revealing wonder,
Filling all above and under;
If in light you make a schism,
'Tis the deepest in the prism.
   The room looks common; but the fact is
'Tis a cell of magic practice,
So disguised by common daylight,
By its disenchanting grey light,
Only spirit-eyes, mesmeric,
See its glories esoteric.
There, that case against the wall,
Glowingly purpureal!
A piano to the prosy—
Not to us in twilight rosy:
'Tis a cave where Nereids lie.
Naiads, Dryads, Oreads sigh,
Dreaming of the time when they
Danced in forest and in bay.
In that chest before your eyes,
Nature's self enchanted lies;
Awful hills and midnight woods;
Sunny rains in solitudes;
Deserts of unbounded longing;
Blessed visions, gladness thronging;
   All this globe of life unfoldeth
In phantom forms that coffer holdeth.
True, unseen; for 'tis enchanted—
What is that but kept till wanted?
Do you hear that voice of singing?
'Tis the enchantress that is flinging
Spells around her baby's riot,
Music's oil the waves to quiet:
She at once can disenchant them,
To a lover's wish to grant them;

She can make the treasure casket
Yield its riches, as that basket
Yielded up the gathered flowers;
Yet its mines, and fields, and bowers,
Full remain, as mother Earth
Never tired of giving birth.
  Do you doubt me? Wait till night
Brings black hours and white delight;
Then, as now, your limbs outstretching,
Yield yourself to her bewitching.
She will bring a book of spells
Writ like crabbed oracles;
Wherewith necromantic fingers
Raise the ghosts of parted singers:
Straight your senses will be bound
In a net of torrent sound.
For it is a silent fountain,
Fed by springs from unseen mountain.
  Till with gestures cabalistic,
Crossing, lining figures mystic,
(Diagram most mathematic,
Simple to these signs erratic,)
O'er the seals her quick hands going
Loose the rills and set them flowing:
Pent up music rushing out
Bathes thy spirit all about;
Spell-bound nature, freed again,
Joyous revels in thy brain.
  On a mountain-top you stand,
Looking o'er a sunny land;
Giant forces marching slow,
Rank on rank, the great hills go,
On and on without a stay,
Melting in the blue away.
Wondrous light, more wondrous shading;
High relief in faintness fading;
Branching streams, like silver veins,
Meet and part in dells and plains.
There a woody hollow lies,
Dumb with love, and bright with eyes;
Moorland tracks of broken ground
Rising o'er, it all around:
Traveller climbing from the grove
Needs the tender heavens above.
"Ah, my pictured life," you cry,
"Fading into sea and sky!"

Lost in thought that gently grieves you,
All the fairy landscape leaves you;
Sinks the sadness into rest,
Ripple-like on water's breast;
Mother's bosom rests the daughter,—
Grief the ripple, Love the water.
All the past is strangely blended
In a mist of colours splendid,
But chaotic as to form,
An unfeatured beauty-storm.
  Wakes within, the ancient mind
For a gloriousness defined:
As she sought and knew your pleasure,—
Wiling with a dancing measure,
Underneath your closed eyes
She calls the shapes of clouded skies;
White forms flushing hyacinthine
Twine in curvings labyrinthine;
Seem with godlike graceful feet,
For such mazy motion meet,
To press from air each lambent note,
On whose throbbing fire they float;
With an airy wishful gait
On each others' motion wait;
Naked arms and vesture free
Fill up the dance of harmony.
  Gone the measure polyhedral!
Springs aloft a high cathedral;
Every arch, like praying arms
Upward flung in love's alarms,
Knit by clasped hands o'erhead,
Heaves to heaven the weight of dread.
Underneath thee, like a cloud,
Gathers music, dim not loud,
Swells thy bosom with devotion,
Floats thee like a wave of ocean;
Vanishes the pile away,—
In heaven thou kneelest down to pray.
  Let the sounds but reach thy heart,
Straight thyself magician art;
Walkest open-eyed through earth;
Seest wonders in their birth,
Whence they come and whither go;
Thou thyself exalted so,
Nature's consciousness, whereby
On herself she turns her eye.

Only heed thou worship God;
Else thou stalkest on thy sod,
Puppet-god of picture-world,
For thy foolish gaze unfurled;
Mirror-thing of things below thee.
Thy own self can never know thee;
Not a high and holy actor;
A reflector, and refractor;
Helpless in thy gift of light,
Self-consuming into night.
   Lasting yet the roseate glory!
I must hasten with my story
Of the little room's true features,
Seldom seen by mortal creatures;
Lest my prophet-vision fading
Leave me in the darkness wading.
What are those upon the wall,
Ranged in rows symmetrical?
They are books, an owl would say;
But the owl's night is the day:
Of these too, if you have patience,
I can give you revelations:
Through the walls of Time and Sight,
Doors they are to the Infinite;
Through the limits that embrace us,
Openings to the eternal spaces,
Round us all the noisy day,
Full of silences alway;
Round us all the darksome night,
Ever full of awful light:
And, though closed, may still remind us
There is mystery behind us.
   That, my friend? Now, it is curious,
You should hit upon the spurious!
'Tis a blind, a painted door:
Knock at it for evermore,
Never vision it affords
But its panelled gilded boards;
Behind it lieth nought at all,
But the limy, webby wall.
Oh no, not a painted block—
Not the less a printed mock;
A book, 'tis true; no whit the more
A revealing out-going door.
There are two or three such books
For a while in others' nooks;

Where they should no longer be,
But for reasons known to me.
  Do not open that one though.
It is real; but if you go
Careless to it, as to dance,
You'll see nothing for your glance;
Blankness, deafness, blindness, dumbness,
Soon will stare you to a numbness.
No, my friend; it is not wise
To open doors into the skies,
As into a little study,
Where a feeble brain grows muddy.
Wait till night, and you shall be
Left alone with mystery;
Light this lamp's white softened ray,
(Another wonder by the way,)
Then with humble faith and prayer,
Ope the door with patient care:
Yours be calmness then, and strength
For the sight you see at length.
  Sometimes, after trying vainly,
With much effort, forced, ungainly,
To entice the rugged door
To yield up its wondrous lore,
With a sudden burst of thunder
All its frame is dashed asunder;
The gulfy silence, lightning-fleet,
Shooteth hellward at thy feet.
Take thou heed lest evil terror
Snare thee in a downward error,
Drag thee through the narrow gate,
Give thee up to windy fate,
To be blown for evermore
Up and down without a shore;
For to shun the good as ill
Makes the evil bolder still.
But oftener far the portal opes
With the sound of coming hopes;
On the joy-astonished eyes
Awful heights of glory rise;
Mountains, stars, and dreadful space,
The Eternal's azure face.
In storms of silence self is drowned,
Leaves the soul a gulf profound,
Where new heavens and earth arise,
Rolling seas and arching skies.

Gathers slow a vapour o'er thee
From the ocean-depths before thee:
Lo! the vision all hath vanished,
Thou art left alone and banished;
Shut the door, thou findest, groping,
Without chance of further oping.
Thou must wait until thy soul
Rises nearer to its goal;
Till more childhood strength has given—
Then approach this gate of Heaven:
It will open as before,
Yielding wonders, yet in store
For thee, if thou wilt turn to good
Things already understood.
  Why I let such useless lumber
Useful bookshelves so encumber?
I will tell thee; for thy question
Of wonders brings me to the best one.
There's a future wonder, may be—
Sure a present magic baby;
(Patience, friend, I know your looks—
What has that to do with books?)
With her sounds of molten speech
Quick a parent's heart to reach,
Though uncoined to words sedate,
Or even to sounds articulate;
Yet sweeter than the music's flowing,
Which doth set her music going.
Now our highest wonder-duty
Is with this same wonder-beauty;
How, with culture high and steady,
To unfold a magic-lady;
How to keep her full of wonder
At all things above and under;
Her from childhood never part,
Change the brain, but keep the heart.
She is God's child all the time;
On all the hours the child must climb,
As on steps of shining stairs
Leading up the path of prayers.
So one lesson from our looks,
Must be this: to honour books,
As a strange and mystic band
Which she cannot understand;
Scarce to touch them without fear,
Never, but when I am near,

As a priest, to temple-rite
Leading in the acolyte.
But when she has older grown,
And can see a difference shown,
   She must learn, 'tis not *appearing*
Makes a book fit for revering;
To distinguish and divide
'Twixt the form and soul inside;
That a book is more than boards,
Leaves and words in gathered hordes,
Which no greater good can do man
Than the goblin hollow woman,
Or a pump without a well,
Or priest without an oracle.
Form is worthless, save it be
Type of an infinity;
Sign of something present, true,
Though unopened to the view,
Heady in its bosom holding
What it will be aye unfolding,
Never uttering but in part,
From an unexhausted heart.
Sight convincing to her mind,
I will separate kind from kind,
Take those books, though honoured by her
Lay them on the study fire,
For their form's sake somewhat tender,
Yet consume them to a cinder;
Years of reverence shall not save them
From the greedy flames that crave them.
You shall see this slight Immortal,
Half-way yet within life's portal;
Gathering gladness, she looks back,
Streams it forward on her track;
Wanders ever in the dance
Of her own sweet radiance.
Though the glory cease to burn,
Inward only it will turn;
Make her hidden being bright,
Make herself a lamp of light;
And a second gate of birth
Will take her to another earth.
   But, my friend, I've rattled plenty
To suffice for mornings twenty;
And I must not toss you longer
On this torrent waxing stronger.

Other things, past contradiction,
Here would prove I spoke no fiction,
Did I lead them up, choragic,
To reveal their nature magic.
There is that machine, glass-masked,
With continual questions tasked,
Ticking with untiring rock:
It is called an eight-day clock.
But to me the thing appears
Made for winding up the years,
Drawing on, fast as it can,
The day when comes the Son of Man.
  On the sea the sunshine broods,
And the shining tops of woods;
We will leave these oracles,
Finding others 'mid the hills.

  SYMPATHY.

  Grief held me silent in my seat,
  I neither moved nor smiled:
Joy held her silent at my feet,
  My little lily-child.
  She raised her face; she seemed to feel
  That she was left outside;
She said one word with childish zeal
  That would not be denied.
  Twice more my name, with infant grace;
  Sole word her lips could mould!
Her face was pulling at my face—
  She was but ten months old.
  I know not what were my replies—
  I thought: dost Thou, O God,
Need ever thy poor children's eyes,
  To ease thee of thy load?
  They find not Thee in evil case,
  But, raised in sorrow wild,
Bring down from visiting thy face
  The calmness of a child.
  Thou art the depth of Heaven above—
  The springing well in her;
Not Father only in thy love,
  But daily minister.
  And this is how the comfort slid
  From her to me the while,—
It was thy present face that did
  Smile on me from her smile.

LITTLE ELFIE.

I have an elfish maiden child;
  She is not two years old;
Through windy locks her eyes gleam wild,
  With glances shy and bold.
  Like little imps, her tiny hands
  Dart out and push and take;
Chide her—a trembling thing she stands,
  And like two leaves they shake.
  But to her mind a minute gone
  Is like a year ago;
So when you lift your eyes anon,
  They're at it, to and fro.
  Sometimes, though not oppressed with thought,
  She has her sleepless fits;
Then to my room in blanket brought,
  In round-backed chair she sits;
  Where, if by chance in graver mood,
  A hermit she appears,
Seated in cave of ancient wood,
  Grown very still with years.
  Then suddenly the pope she is,
  A playful one, I know;
For up and down, now that, now this,
  Her feet like plash-mill go.
  Why like the pope? She's at it yet,
  Her knee-joints flail-like go:
Unthinking man! it is to let
  Her mother kiss each toe.
  But if I turn away and write,
  Then sudden look around,
I almost tremble; tall and white
  She stands upon the ground.
  In long night-gown, a tiny ghost,
  She stands unmoving there;
Or if she moves, my wits were lost
  To meet her on the stair!
  O Elfie, make no haste to lose
  Thy lack of conscious sense;
Thou hast the best gift I could choose,
  A God-like confidence.

THE THANK OFFERING.

  My little child receives my gift,
  A simple piece of bread;
But to her mouth she doth not lift
  The love in bread conveyed,

Till on my lips, unerring, swift,
  The morsel first is laid.
   This is her grace before her food,
  This her libation poured;
Uplift, like offering Aaron good
  Heaved up unto the Lord;
More riches in the thanks than could
  A thousand gifts afford!
   My Father, every gift of thine,
  Teach me to lift to Thee;
Not else know I the love divine,
  With which it comes to me;
Not else the tenfold gift is mine
  Of taking thankfully.
   Yea, all my being I would lift,
  An offering of me;
Then only truly mine the gift,
  When so received by Thee;
Then shall I go, rejoicing, swift,
  Through thine Eternity.

THE BURNT OFFERING.

  Is there a man on earth, who, every night,
When the day hath exhausted each strong limb,
Lays him upon his bed in chamber dim,
And his heart straightway trembling with delight,
Begins to burn up towards the vaulted height
Of the great peace that overshadows him?
Like flakes of fire his thoughts within him swim,
Till all his soul is radiant, blazing bright.
The great earth under him an altar is,
Upon whose top a sacrifice he lies,
Burning to God up through the nightly skies,
Whose love, warm-brooding o'er him, kindled his;
Until his flaming thoughts, consumed, expire,
Sleep's ashes covering the yet glowing fire.

FOUR SONNETS

  Inscribed to S.F.S., because the second is about her father.
I.
  They say that lonely sorrows do not chance.
I think it true, and that the cause I know:
A sorrow glideth in a funeral show
Easier than if it broke into a dance.
But I think too, that joy doth joy enhance
As often as an added grief brings low;
And if keen-eyed to see the flowers that grow,
As keen of nerve to feel the thorns that lance

The foot that must walk naked in one way—
Blest by the lily, white from toils and fears,
Oftener than wounded by the thistle-spears,
We should walk upright, bold, and earnest-gay.
I'll tell you how it fared with me one day
After noon in a world, so-called, of tears.
   II.
   I went to listen to my teacher friend.
O Friend above, thanks for the friend below!
Who having been made wise, deep things to know,
With brooding spirit over them doth bend,
Until they waken words, as wings, to send
Their seeds far forth, seeking a place to grow.
The lesson past, with quiet foot I go,
And towards his silent room, expectant wend,
Seeking a blessing, even leave to dwell
For some eternal minutes in his eyes.
And he smiled on me in his loving wise;
His hand spoke friendship, satisfied me well;
My presence was some pleasure, I could tell.
Then forth we went beneath the smoky skies.
   III.
   I, strengthened, left him. Next in a close place,
Mid houses crowded, dingy, barred, and high,
Where men live not except to sell and buy,
To me, leaving a doorway, came a grace.
(Surely from heaven she came, though all that race
Walketh on human feet beneath the sky.)
I, going on, beheld not who was nigh,
When a sweet girl looked up into my face
With earnest eyes, most maidenly sedate—
Looked up to me, as I to him did look:
'Twas much to me whom sometimes men mistook.
She asked me where we dwelt, that she might wait
Upon us there. I told her, and elate,
Went on my way to seek another nook.
   IV.
   And there I found him whom I went to find,
A man of noble make and head uplift,
Of equal carriage, Nature's bounteous gift;
For in no shelter had his generous mind
Grown flowers that need the winds, rough not unkind.
The joiner's bench taught him, with judgment swift,
Seen things to fashion, unseen things to sift;
From all his face a living soul outshined,
Telling of strength and inward quietude;

His great hand shook mine greatly, and his eyes
Looked straight in mine with spiritual replies:
I left him, rich with overflowing good.
Such joys within two hours of happy mood,
Met me beneath the everlasting skies.
SONNET.
(Exodus xxxiii. 18-23.)
"I do beseech Thee, God, show me thy face."
"Come up to me in Sinai on the morn:
Thou shalt behold as much as may be borne."
And Moses on a rock stood lone in space.
From Sinai's top, the vaporous, thunderous place,
God passed in clouds, an earthly garment worn
To hide, and thus reveal. In love, not scorn,
He put him in a cleft in the rock's base,
Covered him with his hand, his eyes to screen,
Then passed, and showed his back through mists of years.
Ah, Moses! had He turned, and hadst thou seen
The pale face crowned with thorns, baptized with tears,
The eyes of the true man, by men belied,
Thou hadst beheld God's face, and straightway died.
EIGHTEEN SONNETS,
About Jesus.
I.
If Thou hadst been a sculptor, what a race
Of forms divine had ever preached to men!
Lo, I behold thy brow, all glorious then,
(Its reflex dawning on the statue's face)
Bringing its Thought to birth in human grace,
The soul of the grand form, upstarting, when
Thou openest thus thy mysteries to our ken,
Striking a marble window through blind space.
But God, who mouldeth in life-plastic clay,
Flashing his thoughts from men with living eyes,
Not from still marble forms, changeless alway,
Breathed forth his human self in human guise:
Thou didst appear, walking unknown abroad,
The son of man, the human, subject God.
II.
"There, Buonarotti, stands thy statue. Take
Possession of the form; inherit it;
Go forth upon the earth in likeness fit;
As with a trumpet-cry at morning, wake
The sleeping nations; with light's terror, shake
The slumber from their hearts; and, where they sit,
Let them leap up aghast, as at a pit

Agape beneath." I hear him answer make:
"Alas! I dare not; I could not inform
That image; I revered as I did trace;
I will not dim the glory of its grace,
Nor with a feeble spirit mock the enorm
Strength on its brow." Thou cam'st, God's thought thy form,
Living the large significance of thy face.

III.

Some men I have beheld with wonderment,
Noble in form and feature, God's design,
In whom the thought must search, as in a mine,
For that live soul of theirs, by which they went
Thus walking on the earth. And I have bent
Frequent regard on women, who gave sign
That God willed Beauty, when He drew the line
That shaped each float and fold of Beauty's tent;
But the soul, drawing up in little space,
Thus left the form all staring, self-dismayed,
A vacant sign of what might be the grace
If mind swelled up, and filled the plan displayed:
Each curve and shade of thy pure form were Thine,
Thy very hair replete with the divine.

IV.

If Thou hadst been a painter, what fresh looks,
What shining of pent glories, what new grace
Had burst upon us from the great Earth's face!
How had we read, as in new-languaged books,
Clear love of God in lone retreating nooks!
A lily, as thy hand its form would trace,
Were plainly seen God's child, of lower race;
And, O my heart, blue hills! and grassy brooks!
Thy soul lay to all undulations bare,
Answering in waves. Each morn the sun did rise,
And God's world woke beneath life-giving skies,
Thou sawest clear thy Father's meanings there;
'Mid Earth's Ideal, and expressions rare,
The ideal Man, with the eternal eyes.

V.

But I have looked on pictures made by man,
Wherein, at first, appeared but chaos wild;
So high the art transcended, it beguiled
The eye as formless, and without a plan;
Until the spirit, brooding o'er, began
To see a purpose rise, like mountains piled,
When God said: Let the dry earth, undefiled,
Rise from the waves: it rose in twilight wan.

And so I fear thy pictures were too strange
For us to pierce beyond their outmost look;
A vapour and a darkness; a sealed book;
An atmosphere too high for wings to range:
At God's designs our spirits pale and change,
Trembling as at a void, thought cannot brook.
   VI.
   And is not Earth thy living picture, where
Thou utterest beauty, simple and profound,
In the same form by wondrous union bound;
Where one may see the first step of the stair,
And not the next, for brooding vapours there?
And God is well content the starry round
Should wake the infant's inarticulate sound,
Or lofty song from bursting heart of prayer.
And so all men of low or lofty mind,
Who in their hearts hear thy unspoken word,
Have lessons low or lofty, to their kind,
In these thy living shows of beauty, Lord;
While the child's heart that simply childlike is,
Knows that the Father's face looks full in his.
   VII.
   If Thou hadst been a Poet! On my heart
The thought dashed. It recoiled, as, with the gift,
Light-blinded, and joy-saddened, so bereft.
And the hot fountain-tears, with sudden start,
Thronged to mine eyes, as if with that same smart
The husk of vision had in twain been cleft,
Its hidden soul in naked beauty left,
And we beheld thee, Nature, as thou art.
O Poet, Poet, Poet! at thy feet
I should have lien, sainted with listening;
My pulses answering aye, in rhythmic beat,
Each parting word that with melodious wing
Moved on, creating still my being sweet;
My soul thy harp, thy word the quivering string.
   VIII.
   Thou wouldst have led us through the twilight land
Where spirit shows by form, form is refined
Away to spirit by transfiguring mind,
Till they are one, and in the morn we stand;
Treading thy footsteps, children, hand in hand,
With sense divinely growing, till, combined,
We heard the music of the planets wind
In harmony with billows on the strand;
Till, one with Earth and all God's utterance,

We hardly knew whether the sun outspake,
Or a glad sunshine from our spirits brake;
Whether we think, or windy leaflets dance:
Alas, O Poet Leader! for this good,
Thou wert God's tragedy, writ in tears and blood.
   IX.
   So if Thou hadst been scorned in human eyes,
Too bright and near to be a glory then;
If as Truth's artist, Thou hadst been to men
A setter forth of strange divinities;
To after times, Thou, born in midday skies,
A sun, high up, out-blazing sudden, when
Its light had had its centuries eight and ten
To travel through the wretched void that lies
'Twixt souls and truth, hadst been a Love and Fear,
Worshipped on high from Magian's mountain-crest,
And all night long symbol'd by lamp-flames clear;
Thy sign, a star upon thy people's breast,
Where now a strange mysterious shape doth lie,
That once barred out the sun in noontide sky.
   X.
   But as Thou earnest forth to bring the Poor,
Whose hearts were nearer faith and verity,
Spiritual childhood, thy philosophy,—
So taught'st the A, B, C of heavenly lore;
Because Thou sat'st not, lonely evermore,
With mighty thoughts informing language high;
But, walking in thy poem continually,
Didst utter acts, of all true forms the core;
Instead of parchment, writing on the soul
High thoughts and aspirations, being so
Thine own ideal; Poet and Poem, lo!
One indivisible; Thou didst reach thy goal
Triumphant, but with little of acclaim,
Even from thine own, escaping not their blame.
   XI.
   The eye was shut in men; the hearing ear
Dull unto deafness; nought but earthly things
Had credence; and no highest art that flings
A spirit radiance from it, like the spear
Of the ice-pointed mountain, lifted clear
In the nigh sunrise, had made skyey springs
Of light in the clouds of dull imaginings:
Vain were the painter or the sculptor here.
Give man the listening heart, the seeing eye;
Give life; let sea-derived fountain well,

Within his spirit, infant waves, to tell
Of the far ocean-mysteries that lie
Silent upon the horizon,—evermore
Falling in voices on the human shore.
  XII.

  So highest poets, painters, owe to Thee
Their being and disciples; none were there,
Hadst Thou not been; Thou art the centre where
The Truth did find an infinite form; and she
Left not the earth again, but made it be
One of her robing rooms, where she doth wear
All forms of revelation. Artists bear
Tapers in acolyte humility.
O Poet! Painter! soul of all! thy art
Went forth in making artists. Pictures? No;
But painters, who in love should ever show
To earnest men glad secrets from God's heart.
So, in the desert, grass and wild flowers start,
When through the sand the living waters go.
  XIII.

  So, as Thou wert the seed and not the flower,
Having no form or comeliness, in chief
Sharing thy thoughts with thine acquaintance Grief;
Thou wert despised, rejected in thine hour
Of loneliness and God-triumphant power.
Oh, not three days alone, glad slumber brief,
That from thy travail brought Thee sweet relief,
Lay'st Thou, outworn, beneath thy stony bower;
But three and thirty years, a living seed,
Thy body lay as in a grave indeed;
A heavenly germ dropt in a desert wide;
Buried in fallow soil of grief and need;
'Mid earthquake-storms of fiercest hate and pride,
By woman's tears bedewed and glorified.
  XIV.

  All divine artists, humble, filial,
Turn therefore unto Thee, the poet's sun;
First-born of God's creation, only done
When from Thee, centre-form, the veil did fall,
And Thou, symbol of all, heart, coronal,
The highest Life with noblest Form made one,
To do thy Father's bidding hadst begun;
The living germ in this strange planet-ball,
Even as thy form in mind of striving saint.
So, as the one Ideal, beyond taint,
Thy radiance unto all some shade doth yield,

In every splendour shadowy revealed:
But when, by word or hand, Thee one would paint,
Power falls down straightway, speechless, dim-eyed, faint.
   XV.

   Men may pursue the Beautiful, while they
Love not the Good, the life of all the Fair;
Keen-eyed for beauty, they will find it where
The darkness of their eyes hath power to slay
The vision of the good in beauty's ray,
Though fruits the same life-giving branches bear.
So in a statue they will see the rare
Beauty of thought moulded of dull crude clay,
While loving joys nor prayer their souls expand.
So Thou didst mould thy thoughts in Life not Art;
Teaching with human voice, and eye, and hand,
That none the beauty from the truth might part:
Their oneness in thy flesh we joyous hail—
The Holy of Holies' cloud-illumined veil!
   XVI.

   And yet I fear lest men who read these lines,
Should judge of them as if they wholly spake
The love I bear Thee and thy holy sake;
Saying: "He doth the high name wrong who twines
Earth's highest aim with Him, and thus combines
Jesus and Art." But I my refuge make
In what the Word said: "Man his life shall take
From every word:" in Art God first designs,—
He spoke the word. And let me humbly speak
My faith, that Art is nothing to the act,
Lowliest, that to the Truth bears witness meek,
Renownless, even unknown, but yet a fact:
The glory of thy childhood and thy youth,
Was not that Thou didst show, but didst the Truth.
   XVII

   The highest marble Sorrow vanishes
Before a weeping child.[2] The one doth seem,
The other is. And wherefore do we dream,
But that we live? So I rejoice in this,
That Thou didst cast Thyself, in all the bliss
Of conscious strength, into Life's torrent stream,
(Thy deeds fresh life-springs that with blessings teem)
Acting, not painting rainbows o'er its hiss.
Forgive me, Lord, if in these verses lie
Mean thoughts, and stains of my infirmity;
Full well I know that if they were as high
In holy song as prophet's ecstasy,

'Tis more to Thee than this, if I, ah me!
Speak gently to a child for love of Thee.
 [Footnote 2: John Sterling.]
 XVIII.
  Thou art before me, and I see no more
Pilate or soldiers, but the purple flung
Around the naked form the scourge had wrung,
To naked Truth thus witnessing, before
The False and trembling True. As on the shore
Of infinite Love and Truth, I kneel among
Thy footprints on that pavement; and my tongue
Would, but for reverence, cry: "If Thou set'st store
By feeble homage, Witness to the Truth,
Thou art the King, crowned by thy witnessing!"
I die in soul, and fall down worshipping.
Art glories vanish, vapours of the morn.
Never but Thee was there a man in sooth,
Never a true crown but thy crown of thorn.
 DEATH AND BIRTH.
 A Symbol.
  [Sidenote: *He looks from his window on the midnight town.*]
  'Tis the midnight hour; I heard
The city clocks give out the word.
Seldom are the lamp-rays shed
On the quick foot-farer's head,
As I sit at my window old,
Looking out into the cold,
Down along the narrowing street
Stretching out below my feet,
From base of this primeval block,
My old home's foundation rock.
 [Sidenote: *He renounces Beauty the body for Truth the soul.*]
  How her windows are uplighted!
God in heaven! for this I slighted,
Star-profound immensity
Brooding ever in the sky!
What an earthly constellation
Fills those chambers with vibration!
Fleeting, gliding, weaving, parting;
Light of jewels! flash of eyes!
Meeting, changing, wreathing, darting,
In a cloud of rainbow-dyes.
Soul of light, her eyes are floating
Hither, thither, through the cloud,
Wandering planets, seeking, noting
Chosen stars amid the crowd.

Who, as centre-source of motion
Draws those dark orbs' spirit-ocean?
All the orbs on which they turn
Sudden with shooting radiance burn;
Mine I felt grow dim with sheen,
Sending tribute to their queen:
Queen of all the slaves of show—
Queen of Truth's free nobles—no.
She my wandering eyes might chain,
Fill my throbbing burning brain:
Beauty lacking Truth within
Spirit-homage cannot win.
Will is strong, though feeling waver
Like the sea to its enslaver—
Strong as hills that bar the sea
With the word of the decree.
   [Sidenote: *The Resentment of Genius at the thumbscrews of worldly talent.*]
   That passing shadow in the street!
Well I know it, as is meet!
Did he not, before her face,
Seek to brand me with disgrace?
From the chiselled lips of wit
Let the fire-flakes lightly flit,
Scorching as the snow that fell
On the damned in Dante's hell?
With keen-worded opposition,
playful, merciless precision,
Mocking the romance of Youth,
Standing on the sphere of Truth,
He on worldly wisdom's plane
Rolled it to and fro amain.—
Doubtless there it could not lie,
Or walk an orbit but the sky.—
I, who glowed in every limb,
Knowing, could not answer him;
But I longed yet more to be
What I saw he could not see.
So I thank him, for he taught
What his wisdom never sought.
It were sweet to make him burn
With his poverty in turn,
Shaming him in those bright eyes,
Which to him are more than skies!
Whither? whither? Heart, thou knowest
Side by side with him thou goest,

If thou lend thyself to aught
But forgiving, saving thought.
  [Sidenote: *Repentance.*]
  [Sidenote: *The recess of the window a niche, wherein he beholds all the world of his former walk as the picture of a vain slave.*]
  Ah! come in; I need your aid.
Bring-your tools, as then I said.—
There, my friend, build up that niche.
"Pardon me, my lord, but which?"
That, in which I stood this minute;
That one with the picture in it.—
"The window, do you mean, my lord?
Such, few mansions can afford!
Picture is it? 'Tis a show
Picture seldom can bestow!
City palaces and towers,
Forest depths of floating pines,
Sloping gardens, shadowed bowers;
Use with beauty here combines."
True, my friend, seen with your eyes:
But in mine 'tis other quite:
In that niche the dead world lies,
Shadowed over with the night.
In that tomb I'll wall it out;
Where, with silence all about,
Startled only by decay
As the ancient bonds give way,
Sepulchred in all its charms,
Circled in Death's nursing arms,
Mouldering without a cross,
It may feed itself on loss.
  [Sidenote: *The Devil Contempt whistling through the mouth of the Saint Renunciation.*]
  Now go on, lay stone on stone,
I will neither sigh nor moan.—
Whither, whither, Heart of good?
  [Sidenote: *Repentance.*]
  Art thou not, in this thy mood,
One of evil, priestly band,
With dark robes and lifted hand,
Square-faced, stony-visaged men,
In a narrow vaulted den,
Watching, by the cresset dun,
A wild-eyed, pale-faced, staring nun,
Who beholds, as, row by row,
Grows her niche's choking wall,

The blood-red tide of hell below
Surge in billowy rise and fall?
   [Sidenote: Dying unto sin]
   Yet build on; for it is I
To the world would gladly die;
To the hopes and fears it gave me,
To the love that would enslave me,
To the voice of blame it raises,
To the music of its praises,
To its judgments and its favours,
To its cares and its endeavours,
To the traitor-self that opes
Secret gates to cunning hopes;—
Dying unto all this need,
I shall live a life indeed;
Dying unto thee, O Death,
Is to live by God's own breath.
Therefore thus I close my eyes,
Thus I die unto the world;
Thus to me the same world dies,
Laid aside, a map upfurled.
Keep me, God, from poor disdain:
When to light I rise again,
With a new exultant life
Born in sorrow and in strife,
Born of Truth and words divine,
I will see thee yet again,
Dwell in thee, old world of mine,
Aid the life within thy men,
Helping them to die to thee,
And walk with white feet, radiant, free;
Live in thee, not on thy love,
Breathing air from heaven above.
   [Sidenote: *Regret at the memory of Beauty, and Appreciation, and Praise.*]
   Lo! the death-wall grows amain;
And in me triumphant pain
To and fro and outward goes
As I feel my coffin close.—
Ah, alas, some beauties vanish!
Ah, alas, some strength I banish!
Maidens listening with a smile
In confiding eyes, the while
Truths they loved so well to hear
Left my lips. Lo, they draw near!
Lo! I see my forehead crowned
With a coronal of faces,

Where the gleam of living graces
Each to other keeps them bound;
Leaning forward in a throng,
I the centre of their eyes,
Voices mute, that erst in song
Stilled the heart from all but sighs—
Now in thirsty draughts they take
At open eyes and ears, the Truth
Spoken for their love and youth—
Hot, alas! for bare Truth's sake!
There were youths that held by me,
Youths with slightly furrowed brows,
Bent for thought like bended bows;
Youths with souls of high degree
Said that I alone could teach them,
I, one of themselves, could reach them;
I alone had insight nurst,
Cared for Truth and not for Form,
Would not call a man a worm,
Saw God's image in the worst.
And they said my words were strong,
Made their inward longings rise;
Even, of mine, a little song,
Lark-like, rose into the skies.
Here, alas! the self-same folly;
'Twas not for the Truth's sake wholly,
Not for sight of the thing seen,
But for Insight's sake I ween.
Now I die unto all this;
Kiss me, God, with thy cold kiss.
   [Sidenote: *"I dreamed that Allah kissed me, and his kiss was cold."*]
   All self-seeking I forsake;
In my soul a silence make.
There was joy to feel I *could*,
That I had some power of good,
That I was not vainly tost:
Now I'm empty, empty quite;
Fill me, God, or I am lost;
In my spirit shines no light;
All the outer world's wild press
Crushes in my emptiness.
Am I giving all away?
Will the sky be always grey?
Never more this heart of mine
Beat like heart refreshed with wine?

I shall die of misery,
If Thou, God, come not to me.
   [Sidenote: *Dead indeed unto Sin.*]
   Now 'tis finished. So depart
All untruth from out my heart;
All false ways of speaking, thinking;
All false ways of looking, linking;
All that is not true and real,
Tending not to God's Ideal:
Help me—how shall human breath
Word *Thy* meaning in this death!
   [Sidenote: *How is no matter, so that he wake to Life and Sight.*]
   Now come hither. Bring that tool.
Its name I know not; but its use
Written on its shape in full
Tells me it is no abuse
If I strike a hole withal
Through this thick opposed wall.
The rainbow-pavement! Never heed it—
What is that, where light is needed?
Where? I care not; quickest best.
What kind of window would I choose?
Foolish man, what sort of hues
Would you have to paint the East,
When each hill and valley lies
Hungering for the sun to rise?
'Tis an opening that I want;
Let the light in, that is all;
Needful knowledge it will grant.
How to frame the window tall.
Who at morning ever lies
Thinking how to ope his eyes?
This room's eyelids I will ope,
Make a morning as I may;
'Tis the time for work and hope;
Night is waning near the day.
   I bethink me, workman priest;
It were best to pierce the wall
Where the thickness is the least—
Nearer there the light-beams fall,
Sooner with our dark to mix—
That niche where stands the Crucifix.
"The Crucifix! what! impious task!
Wilt thou break into its shrine?
Taint with human the Divine?"
Friend, did Godhead wear a mask

Of the human? or did it
Choose a form for Godhead fit?
   [Sidenote: *The form must yield to the Truth.*]
   Brother with the rugged crown
Won by being all divine,
This my form may come to Thine:
Gently thus I lift Thee down;
Lovingly, O marble cold,
Thee with human hands I fold,
And I set Thee thus aside,
Human rightly deified!
God, by manhood glorified!
   [Sidenote: *Nothing less than the Cross would satisfy the Godhead for its own assertion and vindication.*]
   Thinkest thou that Christ did stand
Shutting God from out the land?
Hiding from His children's eyes
Dayspring in the holy skies?
Stood He not with loving eye
On one side, to bring us nigh?
"Doth this form offend you still?
God is greater than you see;
If you seek to do His will,
He will lead you unto me."
Then the tender Brother's grace
Leads us to the Father's face.
As His parting form withdrew,
Burst His Spirit on the view.
Form completest, radiant white,
Sometimes must give way for light,
When the eye, itself obscure,
Stead of form is needing cure:
Washed at morning's sunny brim
From the mists that make it dim,
Set thou up the form again,
And its light will reach the brain.
For the Truth is Form allowed,
For the glory is the cloud;
But the single eye alone
Sees with light that is its own,
From primeval fountain-head
Flowing ere the sun was made;
Such alone can be regaled
With the Truth by form unveiled;
To such an eye his form will be
Gushing orb of glory free.

[Sidenote: *Striving*.]
　Stroke on stroke! The frescoed plaster
Clashes downward, fast and faster.
Now the first stone disengages;
Now a second that for ages
Bested there as in a rock
Yields to the repeated shock.
Hark! I heard an outside stone
Down the rough rock rumbling thrown!
　[Sidenote: *Longing*.]
　Haste thee, haste! I am athirst
To behold young Morning, nurst
In the lap of ancient Night,
Growing visibly to light.
There! thank God! a faint light-beam!
There! God bless that little stream
Of cool morning air that made
A rippling on my burning head!
　[Sidenote: *Alive unto God.*]
　Now! the stone is outward flung,
And the Universe hath sprung
Inward on my soul and brain!
　[Sidenote: *A New Life*.]
　I am living once again!
Out of sorrow, out of strife,
Spring aloft to higher life;
Parted by no awful cleft
From the life that I have left;
Only I myself grown purer
See its good so much the surer,
See its ill with hopeful eye,
Frown more seldom, oftener sigh.
Dying truly is no loss,
For to wings hath grown the cross.
Dear the pain of giving up,
If Christ enter in and sup.
Joy to empty all the heart,
That there may be room for Him!
Faintness cometh, soon to part,
For He fills me to the brim.
I have all things now and more;
All that I possessed before;
In a calmer holier sense,
Free from vanity's pretence;
And a consciousness of bliss,
Wholly mine, by being His.

I am nearer to the end
Whither all my longings tend.
His love in all the bliss I had,
Unknown, was that which made me glad;
And will shine with glory more,
In the forms it took before.
  [Sidenote: *Beauty returned with Truth.*]
  Lo! the eastern vapours crack
With the sunshine at their back!
Lo! the eastern glaciers shine
In the dazzling light divine!
Lo! the far-off mountains lifting
Snow-capt summits in the sky!
Where all night the storm was drifting,
Whiteness resteth silently!
Glorious mountains! God's own places!
Surely man upon their faces
Climbeth upward nearer Thee
Dwelling in Light's Obscurity!
Mystic wonders! hope and fear
Move together at your sight.
  [Sidenote: *Silence and Thought.*]
  That one precipice, whose height
I can mete by inches here,
Is a thousand fathoms quite.
I must journey to your foot,
Grow on you as on my root;
Feed upon your silent speech,
Awful air, and wind, and thunder,
Shades, and solitudes, and wonder;
  [Sidenote: *The Realities of existence must seize on his soul.*]
  Distances that lengthening roll
Onward, on, beyond Thought's reach,
Widening, widening on the view;
Till the silence touch my soul,
Growing calm and vast like you.
I will meet Christ on the mountains;
Dwell there with my God and Truth;
  [Sidenote: *Baptism.*]
  Drink cold water from their fountains,
Baptism of an inward youth.
Then return when years are by,
To teach a great humility;
  [Sidenote: *Future mission.*]
  To aspiring youth to show
What a hope to them is given:

Heaven and Earth at one to know;
On the Earth to live in Heaven;
Winning thus the hearts of Earth
To die into the Heavenly Birth.
 EARLY POEMS.
  LONGING.
  Away from the city's herds!
  Away from the noisy street!
Away from the storm of words,
  Where hateful and hating meet!
  Away from the vapour grey,
  That like a boding of ill
Is blotting the morning gay,
  And gathers and darkens still!
  Away from the stupid book!
 For, like the fog's weary rest,
With anger dull it fills each nook
  Of my aching and misty breast.
  Over some shining shore,
  There hangeth a space of blue;
A parting 'mid thin clouds hoar
  Where the sunlight is falling through.
  The glad waves are kissing the shore
  Rejoice, and tell it for ever;
The boat glides on, while its oar
  Is flashing out of the river.
  Oh to be there with thee!
  Thou and I only, my love!
The sparkling, sands and the sea!
  And the sunshine of God above!
  MY EYES MAKE PICTURES.
  "My eyes make pictures, when they are shut."
  COLERIDGE.
  Fair morn, I bring my greeting
  To lofty skies, and pale,
Save where cloud-shreds are fleeting
  Before the driving gale,
The weary branches tossing,
  Careless of autumn's grief,
Shadow and sunlight crossing
  On each earth-spotted leaf.
  I will escape their grieving;
  And so I close my eyes,
And see the light boat heaving
  Where the billows fall and rise;
I see the sunlight glancing

Upon its silvery sail,
Where a youth's wild heart is dancing,
  And a maiden growing pale.
  And I am quietly pacing
The smooth stones o'er and o'er,
Where the merry waves are chasing
  Each other to the shore.
Words come to me while listening
  Where the rocks and waters meet,
And the little shells are glistening
  In sand-pools at my feet.
  Away! the white sail gleaming!
  Again I close my eyes,
And the autumn light is streaming
  From pale blue cloudless skies;
Upon the lone hill falling
  'Mid the sound of heather-bells,
Where the running stream is calling
  Unto the silent wells.
  Along the pathway lonely,
  My horse and I move slow;
No living thing, save only
  The home-returning crow.
And the moon, so large, is peering
  Up through the white cloud foam;
And I am gladly nearing
  My father's house, my home.
  As I were gently dreaming
  The solemn trees look out;
The hills, the waters seeming
  In still sleep round about;
And in my soul are ringing
  Tones of a spirit-lyre,
As my beloved were singing
  Amid a sister-choir.
  If peace were in my spirit,
  How oft I'd close my eyes,
And all the earth inherit,
  And all the changeful skies!
Thus leave the sermon dreary,
  Thus leave the lonely hearth;
No more a spirit weary—
  A free one of the earth!
  DEATH.
  When, like a garment flung aside at night,
This body lies, or sculpture of cold rest;

When through its shaded windows comes no light,
And the white hands are folded on its breast;
  How will it be with Me, its tenant now?
How shall I feel when first I wander out?
How look on tears from loved eyes falling? How
Look forth upon dim mysteries round about?
  Shall I go forth, slow-floating like a mist,
Over the city with its crowded walls?
Over the trees and meadows where I list?
Over the mountains and their ceaseless falls?
  Over the red cliffs and fantastic rocks;
Over the sea, far-down, fleeting away;
White sea-birds shining, and the billowy shocks
Heaving unheard their shore-besieging spray?
  Or will a veil, o'er all material things
Slow-falling; hide them from the spirit's sight;
Even as the veil which the sun's radiance flings
O'er stars that had been shining all the night?
  And will the spirit be entranced, alone,
Like one in an exalted opium-dream—
Time space, and all their varied dwellers gone;
And sunlight vanished, and all things that seem;
  Thought only waking; thought that doth not own
The lapse of ages, or the change of place;
Thought, in which only that which *is*, is known;
The substance here, the form confined to space?
  Or as a child that sobs itself to sleep,
Wearied with labour which the grown call play,
Waking in smiles as soon as morn doth peep,
Springs up to labour all the joyous day,
  Shall we lie down, weary; and sleep, until
Our souls be cleansed by long and dreamless rest;
Till of repose we drink our thirsting fill,
And wake all peaceful, smiling, pure, and blest?
  I know not—only know one needful thing:
God is; I shall be ever in His view;
I only need strength for the travailing,
Will for the work Thou givest me to do.

LESSONS FOR A CHILD.

I.

  There breathes not a breath of the morning air,
But the spirit of Love is moving there;
Not a trembling leaf on the shadowy tree
Mingles with thousands in harmony;
But the Spirit of God doth make the sound,
And the thoughts of the insect that creepeth around.

And the sunshiny butterflies come and go,
Like beautiful thoughts moving to and fro;
And not a wave of their busy wings
Is unknown to the Spirit that moveth all things.
And the long-mantled moths, that sleep at noon,
And dance in the light of the mystic moon—
All have one being that loves them all;
Not a fly in the spider's web can fall,
But He cares for the spider, and cares for the fly;
And He cares for each little child's smile or sigh.
How it can be, I cannot know;
He is wiser than I; and it must be so.

II.

  The tree-roots met in the spongy ground,
    Looking where water lay;
Because they met, they twined around,
    Embraced, and went their way.
  Drop dashed on drop, as the rain-shower fell,
    Yet they strove not, but joined together;
And they rose from the earth a bright clear well,
    Singing in sunny weather.
  Sound met sound in the wavy air;
    They kissed as sisters true;
Yet, jostling not on their journey fair,
    Each on its own path flew.
  Wind met wind in a garden green;
    Each for its own way pled;
And a trampling whirlwind danced between,
    Till the flower of Love lay dead.

III.

  To C.C.P.
  The bird on the leafy tree,
The bird in the cloudy sky,
The fish in the wavy sea,
The stag on the mountain high,
The albatross asleep
On the waves of the rocking deep,
The bee on its light wing, borne
Over the bending corn,—
What is the thought in the breast
Of the little bird at rest?
What is the thought in the songs
Which the lark in the sky prolongs?
What mean the dolphin's rays,
Winding his watery ways?
What is the thought of the stag,

Stately on yonder crag?
What doth the albatross think,
Dreaming upon the brink
Of the mountain billow, and then
Dreaming down in its glen?
What is the thought of the bee
Fleeting so silently,
Flitting from part to part,
Speedily, gently roving,
Like the love of a thoughtful heart,
Ever at rest, and moving?
What is the life of their thought?
Doth praise their souls employ?
I think it can be nought
But the trembling movement to and fro
Of a bright, life-giving joy.
And the God of cloudless days,
Who souls and hearts doth know,
Taketh their joy for praise,
And biddeth its fountains flow.
  And if, in thy life on earth,
In the chamber, or by the hearth,
Mid the crowded city's tide,
Or high on the lone hill-side,
Thou canst cause a thought of peace,
Or an aching thought to cease,
Or a gleam of joy to burst
On a soul in gladness nurst;
Spare not thy hand, my child;
Though the gladdened should never know
The well-spring amid the wild
Whence the waters of blessing flow.
Find thy reward in the thing
Which thou hast been blest to do;
Let the joy of others cause joy to spring
Up in thy bosom too.
And if the love of a grateful heart
As a rich reward be given,
Lift thou the love of a grateful heart
To the God of Love in Heaven.
  HOPE DEFERRED.
  Summer is come again. The sun is bright,
And the soft wind is breathing. We will joy;
And seeing in each other's eyes the light
Of the same joy, smile hopeful. Our employ
Shall, like the birds', be airy castles, things

Built by gay hopes, and fond imaginings,
Peopling the land within us. We will tell
Of the green hills, and of the silent sea,
And of all summer things that calmly dwell,
A waiting Paradise for you and me.
And if our thoughts should wander upon sorrow,
Yet hope will wait upon the far-off morrow.
   Look on those leaves. It was not Summer's mouth
That breathed that hue upon them. And look there—
On that thin tree. See, through its branches bare,
How low the sun is in the mid-day South!
This day is but a gleam of gladness, flown
Back from the past to tell us what is gone.
For the dead leaves are falling; and our heart,
Which, with the world, is ever changing so,
Gives back, in echoes sad and low,
The rustling sigh wherewith dead leaves depart:
A sound, not murmuring, but faint and wild;
A sorrow for the Past that hath no child,—
No sweet-voiced child with the bright name of Hope.
   We are like you, poor leaves! but have more scope
For sorrow; for our summers pass away
With a slow, year-long, overshadowing decay.
Yea, Spring's first blossom disappears,
Slain by the shadow of the coming years.
   Come round me, my beloved. We will hold
All of us compassed thus: a winter day
Is drawing nigh us. We are growing old;
And, if we be not as a ring enchanted,
About each other's heart, to keep us gay,
The young, who claim that joy which haunted
Our visions once, will push us far away
Into the desolate regions, dim and grey,
Where the sea hath no moaning, and the cloud
No rain of tears, but apathy doth shroud
All being and all time. But, if we keep
Together thus, the tide of youth will sweep
Round us with thousand joyous waves,
As round some palmy island of the deep;
And our youth hover round us like the breath
Of one that sleeps, and sleepeth not to death.
   Thus onward, hand in hand, to parted graves,
The sundered doors into one palace home,
Through age's thickets, faltering, we will go,
If He who leads us, wills it so,
Believing in our youth, and in the Past;

Within us, tending to the last
Love's radiant lamp, which burns in cave or dome;
And, like the lamps that ages long have glowed
In blessed graves, when once the weary load
Of tomb-built years is heaved up and cast,
For youth and immortality, away,
Will flash abroad in open day,
Clear as a star in heaven's blue-vaulted night;
Shining, till then, through every wrinkled fold,
With the Transfiguration's conquering might;
That Youth our faces wondering shall behold,
And shall be glad, not fearing to be old.

THE DEATH OF THE OLD YEAR.

The weary Old Year is dead at last;
His corpse 'mid the ruins of Time is cast,
Where the mouldering wrecks of lost Thought lie,
And the rich-hued blossoms of Passion die
To a withering grass that droops o'er his grave,
The shadowy Titan's refuge cave.
Strange lights from pale moony Memory lie
On the weedy columns beneath its eye;
And strange is the sound of the ghostlike breeze,
In the lingering leaves on the skeleton trees;
And strange is the sound of the falling shower,
When the clouds of dead pain o'er the spirit lower;
Unheard in the home he inhabiteth,
The land where all lost things are gathered by Death.
    Alone I reclined in the closing year;
Voice, nor breathing, nor step was near;
And I said in the weariness of my breast:
Weary Old Year, thou art going to rest;
O weary Old Year, I would I might be
One hour alone in thy dying with thee!
Would thou wert a spirit, whose low lament
Might mix with the sighs from my spirit sent;
For I am weary of man and life;
Weary of restless unchanging strife;
Weary of change that is ever changing;
Weary of thought that is ever ranging,
Ever falling in efforts vain,
Fluttering, upspringing from earth again,
Struggling once more through the darkness to wing
That hangs o'er the birthplace of everything,
And choked yet again in the vapour's breast,
Sinking once more to a helpless rest.
I am weary of tears that scarce are dry,

Ere their founts are filled as the cloud goes by;
Weary of feelings where each in the throng
Mocks at the rest as they crowd along;
Where Pride over all, like a god on high,
Sits enshrined in his self-complacency;
Where Selfishness crawls, the snake-demon of ill,
The least suspected where busiest still;
Where all things evil and painful entwine,
And all in their hate and their sorrow are mine:
O weary Old Year, I would I might be
One hour by thy dying, to weep with thee!
  Peace, the soul's slumber, was round me shed;
The sleep where thought lives, but its pain is dead;
And my musings led me, a spirit-band,
Through the wide realms of their native land;
Till I stood by the couch of the mighty dying,
A lonely shore in the midnight lying.
He lay as if he had laid him to sleep,
And the stars above him their watch did keep;
And the mournful wind with the dreamy sigh,
The homeless wanderer of the sky,
Was the only attendant whose gentle breath
Soothed him yet on the couch of death;
And the dying waves of the heedless sea
Fell at his feet most listlessly.
  But he lay in peace, with his solemn eye
Looking far through the mists of futurity.
A smile gleamed over the death-dew that lay
On his withered cheek as life ebbed away.
A darkness lay on his forehead vast;
But the light of expectancy o'er it was cast,—
A light that shone from the coming day,
Travelling unseen to the East away.
In his cloudy robes that lay shadowing wide,
I stretched myself motionless by his side;
And his eyes with their calm, unimpassioned power,
Soothing my heart like an evening shower,
Led in a spectral, far-billowing train,
The hours of the Past through my spirit again.
  There were fears of evil whose stony eyes
Froze joy in its gushing melodies.
Some floated afar on thy tranquil wave,
And the heart looked up from its search for a grave;
While others as guests to the bosom came,
And left its wild children more sorrow, less shame;
For the death-look parts from their chilling brow,

And they bless the heads that before them bow;
And floating away in the far-off gloom.
Thankfulness follows them to their tomb.
There were Hopes that found not a place to rest
Their foot 'mid the rush of all-ocean's breast;
And home to the sickening heart flew back,
But changed into sorrows upon their track;
And through the moan of the darkening sea
Bearing no leaf from the olive-tree.
There were joys that looked forth with their maiden eyes,
And smiled, and were gone, with a sad surprise;
And the Love of the Earthly, whose beauteous form
Beckoned me on through sunshine and storm;
But when the bounding heart sprang high,
Meeting her smile with a speechless sigh,
The arms sunk home with a painful start,
Clasping a vacancy to the heart.
   And the voice of the dying I seem to hear
But whether his breathing is in mine ear,
Or the sounds of the breaking billows roll
The lingering accents upon my soul,
I know not; but thus they seem to bear
Reproof to my soul for its faint despair:—
Blame not life, it is scarce begun;
Blame not mankind, thyself art one.
And change is holy, oh! blame it never;
Thy soul shall live by its changing ever;
Not the bubbling change of a stagnant pool,
But the change of a river, flowing and full;
Where all that is noble and good will grow
Mightier still as the full tides flow;
Till it joins the hidden, the boundless sea,
Rolling through depths of Eternity.
Blame not thy thought that it cannot reach
That which the Infinite must teach;
Bless thy God that the Word came nigh
To guide thee home to thy native sky,
Where all things are homely and glorious too,
And the children are wondering, and glad, and true.
   And he pointed away to an Eastern star,
That gleamed through his robes o'er the ocean afar;
And I knew that a star had looked o'er the rim
Of my world that lay all dreary and dim;
And was slowly dissolving the darkness deep
Which, like evil nurse, had soothed me to sleep;
And rising higher, and shining clearer,

Would draw the day-spring ever nearer,
Till the sunshine of God burst full on the morn,
And every hill and valley would start
With the joy of light and new gratitude born
To Him who had led me home to His heart;
And all things that lived in my world within
With the gladness of tears to His feet come in;
And the false Self be banished with fiends to dwell
In the gloomiest haunts of his native hell;
And Pride, that ruled like a god above,
Be trod 'neath the feet of triumphant Love.
   And again he pointed across the sea,
And another vision arose in me:
And I knew I walked an ocean of fear,
Yet of safety too, for the Master was near;
And every wave of sorrow or dread,
O'er which strong faith should upraise my head,
Would show from the height of its troubled crest
Still nearer and nearer the Land of Rest.
And when the storm-spray on the wind should arise,
And with tears unbidden should blind mine eyes,
And hide from my vision the Home of Love,
I knew I must look to the star above,
And the mists of Passion would quickly flee,
And the storm would faint to serenity.
   And again it seemed as if words found scope,
The sorrowing words of a farewell Hope:
"I will meet thee again in that deathless land,
Whenever thy foot shall imprint the strand;
And the loveliest things that have here been mine,
Shall there in eternal beauty shine;
For there I shall live and never die,
Part of a glorious Eternity;
For the death of Time is *To be forgot*,
And I go where oblivion entereth not."
   He was dead. He had gone to the rest of his race,
With a sad smile frozen upon his face.
Deadness clouded his eyes. And his death-bell rung,
And my sorrowing thoughts his low requiem sung;
And with trembling steps his worn body cast
In the wide charnel-house of the dreary Past.
Thus met the noble Old Year his end:
Rest him in peace, for he was my friend.
   As my thoughts returned from their wandering,
A voice in my spirit was lingering;

And its sounds were like Spring's first breeze's hum,
When the oak-leaves fall, and the young leaves come:
　Time dieth ever, is ever born:
On the footsteps of night so treadeth the morn;
Shadow and brightness, death and birth,
Chasing each other o'er the round earth.
But the spirit of Time from his tomb is springing,
The dust of decay from his pinions flinging;
Ever renewing his glorious youth,
Scattering around him the dew of Truth.
Oh, let it raise in the desert heart
Fountains and flowers that shall never depart!
This spirit will fill us with thought sublime;
For the *End of God* is the spirit of Time.
　A SONG IN A DREAM.
　I dreamed of a song, I heard it sung;
In the ear that sleeps not its music rung.
And the tones were upheld by harmonies deep,
Where the spirit floated; yea, soared, on their sweep
With each wild unearthly word and tone,
Upward, it knew not whither bound,
In a calm delirium of mystic sound—
Up, where the Genius of Thought alone
Loveth in silence to drink his fill
Of dews that from unknown clouds distil.
A woman's voice the deep echoes awoke,
In the caverns and solitudes of my soul;
But such a voice had never broke
Through the sea of sounds that about us roll,
Choking the ear in the daylight strife.
There was sorrow and triumph, and death and life
In each chord-note of that prophet-song,
Blended in one harmonious throng:
Such a chant, ere my voice has fled from death,
Be it mine to mould of the parting breath.
　A THANKSGIVING.
　I Thank Thee, boundless Giver,
　　That the thoughts Thou givest flow
In sounds that like a river
　　All through the darkness go.
And though few should swell the pleasure,
　　By sharing this my wine,
My heart will clasp its treasure,
　　This secret gift of Thine.
　My heart the joy inherits,
　　And will oft be sung to rest;

And some wandering hoping spirits
  May listen and be blest.
For the sound may break the hours
  In a dark and gloomy mood,
As the wind breaks up the bowers
  Of the brooding sunless wood.
  For every sound of gladness
  Is a prophet-wind that tells
Of a summer without sadness,
  And a love without farewells;
And a heart that hath no ailing,
  And an eye that is not dim,
And a faith that without failing
  Shall be complete in Him.
  And when my heart is mourning,
  The songs it lately gave,
Back to their fount returning,
  Make sweet the bitter wave;
And forth a new stream floweth,
  In sunshine winding fair;
And through the dark wood goeth
  Glad laughter on the air.
  For the heart of man that waketh,
  Yet hath not ceased to dream,
Is the only fount that maketh
  The sweet and bitter stream.
But the sweet will still be flowing
  When the bitter stream is dry,
And glad music only going
  On the breezes of the sky.
  I thank Thee, boundless Giver,
  That the thoughts Thou givest flow
In sounds that like a river
  All through the darkness go.
And though few should swell the pleasure
  By sharing this my wine,
My heart will clasp its treasure,
  This secret gift of Thine.

THE GOSPEL WOMEN.

I.

THE MOTHER MARY.

1.

  Mary, to thee the heart was given
  For infant hand to hold,
Thus clasping, an eternal heaven,
  The great earth in its fold.

He seized the world with tender might,
  By making thee his own;
Thee, lowly queen, whose heavenly height
  Was to thyself unknown.
  He came, all helpless, to thy power,
  For warmth, and love, and birth;
In thy embraces, every hour,
  He grew into the earth.
  And thine the grief, O mother high,
  Which all thy sisters share,
Who keep the gate betwixt the sky
  And this our lower air;
  And unshared sorrows, gathering slow;
  New thoughts within thy heart,
Which through thee like a sword will go,
  And make thee mourn apart.
  For, if a woman bore a son
  That was of angel brood,
Who lifted wings ere day was done,
  And soared from where he stood;
  Strange grief would fill each mother-moan,
  Wild longing, dim, and sore:
"My child! my child! he is my own,
  And yet is mine no more!"
  And thou, O Mary, years on years,
  From child-birth to the cross,
Wast filled with yearnings, filled with fears,
  Keen sense of love and loss.
  His childish thoughts outsoared thy reach;
  His childish tenderness
Had deeper springs than act or speech
  To eye or ear express.
  Strange pangs await thee, mother mild!
  A sorer travail-pain,
Before the spirit of thy child
  Is born in thee again.
  And thou wilt still forbode and dread,
  And loss be still thy fear,
Till form be gone, and, in its stead,
  The very self appear.
  For, when thy Son hath reached his goal,
  His own obedient choice,
Him thou wilt know within thy soul,
  And in his joy rejoice.
  2.

Ah, there He stands! With wondering face
  Old men surround the boy;
The solemn looks, the awful place,
  Restrain the mother's joy.
   In sweet reproach her joy is hid;
   Her trembling voice is low,
Less like the chiding than the chid:
  "How couldst Thou leave us so?"
   Ah, mother! will thy heart mistake,
   Depressed by rising fear,
The answering words that gently break
  The silence of thine ear?
   "Why sought ye me? Did ye not know
   My father's work I do?"
Mother, if He that work forego,
  Not long He cares for you.
   "Why sought ye me?" Ah, mother dear!
   The gulf already opes,
That soon will keep thee to thy fear,
  And part thee from thy hopes.
   A greater work He hath to do,
   Than they can understand;
And therefore mourn the loving few,
  With tears throughout the land.
   3.
   The Lord of life beside them rests;
   They quaff the merry wine;
They do not know, those wedding guests,
  The present power divine.
   Believe, on such a group He smiled,
   Though He might sigh the while;
Believe not, sweet-souled Mary's child
  Was born without a smile.
   He saw the pitchers high upturned,
   The last red drops to pour;
His mother's cheek with triumph burned,
  And expectation wore.
   He knew the prayer her bosom housed,
   He read it in her eyes.
Her hopes in Him sad thoughts have roused,
  Before her words arise.
   "They have no wine," the mother said,
   And ceased while scarce begun;
Her eyes went on, "Lift up thy head,
  Show what Thou art, my Son!"

A vision rose before his eyes,
  The cross, the early tomb,
The people's rage, the darkened skies,
  His unavoided doom.
  "Ah, woman-heart! what end is set
  Common to thee and me?
My hour of honour is not yet,—
  'Twill come too soon for thee."
  And yet his eyes so sweetly shined,
  His voice so gentle grew,
The mother knew the answer kind—
  "Whate'er He sayeth, do."
  The little feast more joyous grew,
  Fast flowed the grapes divine;
Though then, as now, not many knew
  Who made the water wine.
  4.
  "He is beside himself," they said;
 His days, so lonely spent,
Him from the well-known path have led
  In which our fathers went."
  "Thy mother seeks thee." Cried aloud,
  The message finds its way;
He stands within, amidst a crowd,
  She in the open day.
  A flush of light o'erspreads his face,
  And pours from forth his eyes;
He lifts that head, the home of grace,
  Looks round Him, and replies.
  "My mother? brothers? who are they?"
  Hearest thou, Mary mild?
This is a sword that well may slay—
  Disowned by thy child!
  Not so. But, brothers, sisters, hear!
  What says our human Lord?
O mother, did it wound thy ear?
  We thank Him for the word.
  "Who are my friends?" Oh! hear Him say,
  And spread it far and broad.
"My mother, sisters, brothers, they
  Who keep the word of God."
  My brother! Lord of life and me,
  I am inspired with this!
Ah! brother, sister, this must be
  Enough for all amiss.

Yet think not, mother, He denies,
  Or would thy claim destroy;
But glad love lifts more loving eyes
  To Him who made the joy.
  Oh! nearer Him is nearer thee:
  With his obedience bow,
And thou wilt rise with heart set free,
  Yea, twice his mother now.
  5.
  The best of life crowds round its close,
  To light it from the door;
When woman's art no further goes,
  She weeps, and loves the more.
  Howe'er she doubted, in his life,
  And feared his mission's loss,
The mother shares the awful strife,
  And stands beside the cross.
  Mother, the hour of tears is past;
  The sword hath reached thy soul;
No veil of swoon is round thee cast,
  No darkness hides the whole.
  Those are the limbs which thou didst bear;
  Thy arms, they were his rest;
And now those limbs the irons tear,
  And hold Him from thy breast.
  He speaks. With torturing joy the sounds
  Drop burning on thine ear;
The mother-heart, though bleeding, bounds
  Her dying Son to hear.
  Ah! well He knew that not alone
  The cross of pain could tell;
That griefs as bitter as his own
  Around it heave and swell.
  And well He knew what best repose
  Would bring a true relief:
He gave, each to the other, those
  Who shared a common grief.
  "Mother, behold thy son. O friend,
  My mother take for thine."
"Ah, son, he loved thee to the end."
  "Mother, what honour mine!"
  Another son instead, He gave,
  Her crying heart to still.
For him, He went down to the grave,
  Doing his Father's will.

II.
THE WOMAN THAT CRIED IN THE CROWD.
She says within: "It is a man,
　A man of mother born;
She is a woman—I am one,
　Alive this holy morn."
　Filled with his words that flow in light,
　Her heart will break or cry:
A woman's cry bursts forth in might
　Of loving agony.
　"Blessed the womb, Thee, Lord, that bore!
　The breast where Thou hast fed!"
Storm-like those words the silence tore,
　Though words the silence bred.
　He ceases, listens to the cry,
　And knows from whence it springs;
A woman's heart that glad would die
　For this her best of things.
　Yet there is better than the birth
　Of such a mighty son;
Better than know, of all the earth
　Thyself the chosen one.
　"Yea, rather, blessed they that hear,
　And keep the word of God."
The voice was gentle, not severe:
　No answer came abroad.

III.
THE MOTHER OP ZEBEDEE'S CHILDREN.
　Ah mother! for thy children bold,
　But doubtful of thy quest,
Thou begg'st a boon ere it be told,
　Avoiding wisdom's test.
　Though love is strong to bring thee nigh,
　Ambition makes thee doubt;
Ambition dulls the prophet-eye;
　It casts the unseen out.
　Not that in thousands he be one,
　Uplift in lonely state—
Seek great things, mother, for thy son,
　Because the things are great.
　For ill to thee thy prayers avail,
　If granted to thy will;
Ill which thy ignorance would hail,
　Or good thou countedst ill.
　Them thou wouldst see in purple pride,
　Worshipped on every hand;

Their honours mighty but to hide
  The evil of the land.
  Or wouldst thou thank for granted quest,
  Counting thy prayer well heard,
If of the three on Calvary's crest
  They shared the first and third?
  Let them, O mother, safety win;
  They are not safe with thee;
Thy love would shut their glory in;
  His love would set it free.
  God keeps his thrones for men of strength,
  Men that are fit to rule;
Who, in obedience ripe at length,
  Have passed through all his school.
  Yet higher than thy love can dare,
  His love thy sons would set:
They who his cup and baptism share
  May share his kingdom yet.

IV.

THE SYROPHENICIAN WOMAN.

  "Bestow her prayer, and let her go;
  She crieth after us."
Nay, to the dogs ye cast it so;
  Help not a woman thus.
  Their pride, by condescension fed,
  He speaks with truer tongue:
"It is not meet the children's bread
  Should to the dogs be flung."
  She, too, shall share the hurt of good,
  Her spirit, too, be rent,
That these proud men their evil mood
  May see, and so repent.
  And that the hidden faith in her
  May burst in soaring flame,
From childhood truer, holier,
  If birthright not the same.
  If for herself had been her prayer,
  She might have turned away;
But oh! the woman-child she bare
  Was now the demon's prey.
  She crieth still; gainsays no words
  Contempt can hurt withal;
The daughter's woe her strength affords,
  And woe nor strength is small.
  Ill names, of proud religion born,
  She'll wear the worst that comes;

Will clothe her, patient, in their scorn,
  To share the healing crumbs.
  And yet the tone of words so sore
  The words themselves did rue;
His face a gentle sadness wore,
  As if He suffered too.
  Mother, thy agony of care
  He justifies from ill;
Thou wilt not yield?—He grants the prayer
  In fullness of *thy* will.
  Ah Lord! if I my hope of weal
  Upon thy goodness built,
Thy will perchance my will would seal,
  And say: *Be it as thou wilt.*

V.

THE WIDOW OF NAIN.

  Away from living man's abode
  The tides of sorrow sweep,
Bearing a dead man on the road
  To where the weary sleep.
  And down the hill, in sunny state,
  Glad footsteps troop along;
A noble figure walks sedate,
  The centre of the throng.
  The streams flow onward, onward flow,
  Touch, waver, and are still;
And through the parted crowds doth go,
  Before the prayer, the will.
  "Weep not, O mother! Young man, rise!"
  The bearers hear and stay;
Up starts the form; wide flash the eyes;
  With gladness blends dismay.
  The lips would speak, as if they caught
  Some converse sudden broke,
When echoing words the dead man sought,
  And Hades' silence woke.
  The lips would speak. The eyes' wild stare
  Gives place to ordered sight;
The low words die upon the air—
  The soul is dumb with light.
  He brings no news; he has forgot;
  Or saw with vision weak:
Thou seest all our unseen lot,
  And yet thou dost not speak.
  It may be as a mother keeps
  A secret gift in store;

Which if he knew, the child that sleeps,
  That night would sleep no more.
  Oh, thine are all the hills of gold!
  Yet gold Thou gavest none;
Such gifts would leave thy love untold—
  The widow clasps her son.
  No word of hers hath left a trace
  Of uttered joy or grief;
Her tears alone have found a place
  Upon the holy leaf.
  Oh, speechless sure the widow's pain,
  To lose her only boy!
Speechless the flowing tides again
  Of new-made mother's joy!
  Life is triumphant. Joined in one
  The streams flow to the gate;
Death is turned backward to the sun,
  And Life is hailed our Fate.

VI.

THE WOMAN WHOM SATAN HAD BOUND.

  For eighteen years, O patient soul,
  Thine eyes have sought thy grave;
Thou seest not thy other goal,
  Nor who is nigh to save.
  Thou nearest gentle words that wake
  Thy long-forgotten strength;
Thou feelest tender hands that break
  The iron bonds at length.
  Thou knowest life rush swift along
  Thy form bent sadly low;
And up, amidst the wondering throng
  Thou risest firm and slow,
  And seëst him. Erect once more
  In human right divine,
Joyous thou bendest yet before
  The form that lifted thine.
  O Saviour, Thou, long ages gone,
  Didst lift her joyous head:
Now, many hearts are moaning on,
  And bending towards the dead.
  They see not, know not Thou art nigh:
  One day thy word will come;
Will lift the forward-beaming eye,
  And strike the sorrow dumb.
  Thy hand wipes off the stains of time
  Upon the withered face;

Thy old men rise in manhood's prime
  Of dignity and grace.
  Thy women dawn like summer days
  Old winters from among;
Their eyes are filled with youthful rays,
  The voice revives in song.
  All ills of life will melt away
  Like cureless dreams of woe,
When with the dawning of the day
  Themselves the sad dreams go.
  O Lord, Thou art my saviour too:
  I know not what my cure;
But all my best, Thou, Lord, wilt do;
  And hoping I endure.

VII.
THE WOMAN WHO CAME BEHIND HIM IN THE CROWD.
  Near him she stole, rank after rank;
  She feared approach too loud;
She touched his garment's hem, and shrank
  Back in the sheltering crowd.
  A trembling joy goes through her frame:
  Her twelve years' fainting prayer
Is heard at last; she is the same
  As other women there.
  She hears his voice; He looks about.
  Ah! is it kind or good
To bring her secret sorrow out
  Before that multitude?
  With open love, not secret cure,
  The Lord of hearts would bless;
With age-long gladness, deep and sure,
  With wealth of tenderness.
  Her shame can find no shelter meet;
  Their eyes her soul appal:
Forward she sped, and at his feet
  Fell down, and told Him all.
  His presence made a holy place;
  No alien eyes were there;
Her shamed-faced grief found godlike grace;
  More sorrow, tenderer care.
  "Daughter, thy faith hath made thee whole;
  Go, and be well, and glad."
Ah, Lord! if we had faith, our soul
  Not often would be sad.
  Thou knowest all our hidden grief
  Which none but Thee can know;

Thy knowledge, Lord, is our relief;
  Thy love destroys our woe.

VIII.
THE WIDOW WITH THE TWO MITES.

  Here *much* and *little* change their name
   With changing need and time;
But *more* and *less* new judgments claim,
   Where all things are sublime.
  Sickness may be more hale than health,
   And service kingdom high;
Yea, poverty be bounty's wealth,
   To give like God thereby.
  Bring forth your riches,—let them go,
   Nor mourn the lost control;
For if ye hoard them, surely so
   Their rust will reach your soul.
  Cast in your coins; for God delights
   When from wide hands they fall;
But here is one who brings two mites,
   "And yet gives more than all."
  She heard not, she, the mighty praise;
   Went home to care and need:
Perchance the knowledge still delays,
   And yet she has the meed.

IX.
THE WOMEN WHO MINISTERED UNTO HIM.

  They give Him freely all they can,
   They give Him clothes and food;
In this rejoicing, that the Man
   Is not ashamed they should.
  Enough He labours for his hire;
   Yea, nought can pay his pain;
The sole return He doth require
   Is strength to toil again.
  And this, embalmed in truth, they bring,
   By love received as such;
Their little, by his welcoming,
   Transformed into much.

X.
PILATE'S WIFE.

  Strangely thy whispered message ran,
   Almost in form behest!
Why came in dreams the low-born man
   To part thee from thy rest?
  It may be that some spirit fair,
   Who knew not what must be,

Fled in the anguish of his care
  For help for him to thee.
    But rather would I think thee great;
    That rumours upward went,
And pierced the palisades of state
  In which thy rank was pent;
    And that a Roman matron thou,
    Too noble for thy spouse,
The far-heard grandeur must allow,
  And sit with pondering brows.
    And so thy maidens' gathered tale
    For thee with wonder teems;
Thou sleepest, and the prisoner pale
  Returneth in thy dreams.
    And thou hast suffered for his sake
    Sad visions all the night:
One day thou wilt, then first awake,
  Rejoice in his dear light.

XI.

THE WOMAN OF SAMARIA.

  The empty pitcher to the pool
  She bore in listless mood:
In haste she turned; the pitcher full
  Beside the water stood.
    To her was heard the age's prayer:
    He sat upon the brink;
Weary beside the waters fair,
  And yet He could not drink.
    He begged her help. The woman's hand
    Was ready to reply;
From out the old well of the land
  She drew Him plenteously.
    He spake as never man before;
    She stands with open ears;
He spoke of holy days in store,
  Laid bare the vanished years.
    She cannot grapple with her heart,
    Till, in the city's bound,
She cries, to ease the joy-born smart,
  "I have the Master found."
    Her life before was strange and sad;
    Its tale a dreary sound:
Ah! let it go—or good or bad,
  She has the Master found.

XII.
MARY MAGDALENE.
With eyes aglow, and aimless zeal,
  Throughout the land she goes;
Her tones, her motions, all reveal
  A mind without repose.
  She climbs the hills, she haunts the sea,
  By madness tortured, driven;
One hour's forgetfulness would be
  A gift from very heaven.
  The night brings sleep, the sleep distress;
  The torture of the day
Returns as free, in darker dress,
  In more secure dismay.
  No soft-caressing, soothing palm
  Her confidence can raise;
No eye hath loving force to calm
  And draw her answering gaze.
  He comes. He speaks. A light divine
  Dawns gracious in thy soul;
Thou seest love and order shine,—
  His health will make thee whole.
  One wrench of pain, one pang of death,
  And in a faint delight,
Thou liest, waiting for new breath,
  For morning out of night.
  Thou risest up: the earth is fair,
  The wind is cool and free;
As when a dream of mad despair
  Dissolves in ecstasy.
  And, pledge of life and future high,
  Thou seest the Master stand;
The life of love is in his eye,
  Its power is in his hand.
  What matter that the coming time
  Will stain thy virgin name;
Attribute thy distress to crime
  The worst for woman-fame;
  Yea, call that woman Magdalen,
  Whom slow-reviving grace
Turneth at last from evil men
  To seek the Father's face.
  What matters it? The night is gone;
  Right joyous shines the sun;
The same clear sun that always shone
  Ere sorrow had begun.

Oh! any name may come and bide,
 If he be well content
To see not seldom by his side
 Thy head serenely bent.
  Thou, sharing in the awful doom,
  Wilt help thy Lord to die;
And, mourning o'er his empty tomb,
 First share his victory.

XIII.
THE WOMAN IN THE TEMPLE.

 A still dark joy. A sudden face,
  Cold daylight, footsteps, cries;
The temple's naked, shining space,
 Aglare with judging eyes.
  With all thy wild abandoned hair,
  And terror-pallid lips,
Thy blame unclouded to the air,
 Thy honour in eclipse;
  Thy head, thine eyes droop to the ground,
  Thy shrinking soul to hide;
Lest, at its naked windows found,
 Its shame be all descried.
  Another shuts the world apart,
  Low bending to the ground;
And in the silence of his heart,
 Her Father's voice will sound.
  He stoops, He writes upon the ground,
  From all those eyes withdrawn;
The awful silence spreads around
 In that averted dawn.
  With guilty eyes bent downward still,
  With guilty, listless hands,
All idle to the hopeless will,
 She, scorn-bewildered, stands.
  Slow rising to his manly height,
  Fronting the eager eyes,
The righteous Judge lifts up his might,
 The solemn voice replies:
  (What, woman! does He speak for thee?
  For thee the silence stir?)
"Let him who from this sin is free,
 Cast the first stone at her!"
  Upon the death-stained, ashy face,
  The kindling blushes glow:
No greater wonder sure had place
 When Lazarus forth did go!

Astonished, hopeful, growing sad,
  The wide-fixed eyes arose;
She saw the one true friend she had,
  Who loves her though He knows.
  Sick womanhood awakes and cries,
  With voiceless wail replete.
She looks no more; her softening eyes
  Drop big drops at her feet.
  He stoops. In every charnel breast
  Dead conscience rises slow.
They, dumb before the awful guest,
  Turn one by one, and go.
  They are alone. The silence dread
  Closes and deepens round.
Her heart is full, her pride is dead;
  No place for fear is found.
  Hath He not spoken on her side?
  Those cruel men withstood?
Even her shame she would not hide—
  Ah! now she *will* be good.
  He rises. They are gone. But, lo!
  She standeth as before.
"Neither do I condemn thee; go,
  And sin not any more."
  She turned and went. The veil of tears
  Fell over what had been;
Her childhood's dawning heaven appears,
  And kindness makes her clean.
  And all the way, the veil of tears
  Flows from each drooping lid;
No face she sees, no voice she hears,
  Till in her chamber hid.
  And then returns one voice, one face,
  A presence henceforth sure;
The living glory of the place,
  To keep that chamber pure.
  Ah, Lord! with all our faults we come,—
  With love that fails to ill;
With Thee are our accusers dumb,
  With Thee our passions still.
  Ah! more than father's holy grace
  Thy lips and brow afford;
For more than mother's tender face
  We come to Thee, O Lord!

XIV.
MARTHA.

With joyful pride her heart is great:
　Her house, in all the land,
Holds Him who conies, foretold by fate,
　With prophet-voice and hand.
　True, he is poor and lowly born:
　Her woman-soul is proud
To know and hail the coming morn
　Before the eyeless crowd.
　At her poor table will He eat?
　He shall be served there
With honour and devotion meet
　For any king that were.
　'T is all she can; she does not fail;
　Her holy place is his:
The place within the purple veil
　In the great temple is.
　But many crosses she must bear,
　Straight plans are sideways bent;
Do all she can, things will not wear
　The form of her intent.
　With idle hands, by Him unsought,
　Her sister sits at rest;
'Twere better sure she rose, and wrought
　Some service for their guest.
　She feels a wrong. The feeling grows,
　As other cares invade:
Strong in her right, at last she goes
　To claim her sister's aid.
　Ah, Martha! one day thou like her,
　Or here, or far beyond,
Will sit as still, lest, but to stir,
　Should break the charmed bond.

XV.
MARY.

1.

　She sitteth at the Master's feet
　In motionless employ;
Her ears, her heart, her soul complete
　Drinks in the tide of joy.
　She is the Earth, and He the Sun;
　He shineth forth her leaves;
She, in new life from darkness won,
　Gives back what she receives.

Ah! who but she the glory knows
  Of life, pure, high, intense;
Whose holy calm breeds awful shows,
  Transfiguring the sense!
   The life in voice she drinks like wine;
    The Word an echo found;
Her ear the world, where Thought divine
  Incarnate was in sound.
   Her holy eyes, brimful of light,
    Shine all unseen and low;
As if the radiant words all night
  Forth at those orbs would go.
   The opening door reveals a face
    Of anxious household state:
"Car'st thou not, Master, for my case,
  That I alone should wait?"
   Heavy with light, she lifts those eyes
    To Him who calmly heard;
Ready that moment to arise,
  And go, before the word.
   Her fear is banished by his voice,
    Her fluttering hope set free:
"The needful thing is Mary's choice,
  She shall remain with me."
   Oh, joy to every doubting heart,
    Doing the thing it would,
If He, the Holy, take its part,
  And call its choice the good!
   2.
   Not now as then his words are poured
    Into her lonely ears;
But many guests are at the board,
  And many tongues she hears.
   With sacred foot she cometh slow,
    With daring, trembling tread;
With shadowing worship bendeth low
  Above the godlike head.
   The sacred chrism in snowy stone
    A gracious odour sends.
Her little hoard, so slowly grown,
  In one full act she spends.
   She breaks the box, the honoured thing!
    The ointment pours amain;
Her priestly hands anoint her King,
  And He shall live and reign.

They called it waste. Ah, easy well!
  Their love they could endure;
For her, her heart did ache and swell,
  That she forgot the poor.
    She meant it for the coming crown;
    He took it for the doom;
And his obedience laid Him down,
  Crowned in the quiet tomb.

XVI.

THE WOMAN THAT WAS A SINNER

  She washes them with sorrow sweet,
  She wipes them with her hair;
Her kisses soothe the weary feet,
  To all her kisses bare.
    The best of woman, beauty's crown,
    She spends upon his feet;
Her eyes, her lips, her hair, flung down,
  In one devotion meet.
    His face, his words, her heart had woke.
    She judged Him well, in sooth:
Believing Him, her bonds she broke,
  And fled to Him for truth.
    His holy manhood's perfect worth
    Redeems the woman's ill:
Her thanks intense to Him burn forth,
  Who owns her woman still.
    And so, in kisses, ointment, tears,
    And outspread lavish hair,
An earnest of the coming years,
  Ascends her thankful prayer.
    If Mary too her hair did wind
    The holy feet around;
Such tears no virgin eyes could find,
  As this sad woman found.
    And if indeed his wayworn feet
    With love she healed from pain;
This woman found the homage meet,
  And taught it her again.
    The first in grief, ah I let her be,
    And love that springs from woe;
Woe soothed by Him more tenderly
  That sin doth make it flow.
    Simon, such kisses will not soil;
    Her tears are pure as rain;
Her hair—'tis Love unwinds the coil,
  Love and her sister Pain.

If He be kind, for life she cares;
  A light lights up the day;
She to herself a value bears,
  Not yet a castaway.
    And evermore her heart arose,
    And ever sank away;
For something crowned Him o'er her woes,
  More than her best could say.
    Rejoice, sweet sisters, holy, pure,
    Who hardly know her case:
There is no sin but has its cure,
  But finds its answering grace.
    Her heart, although it sinned and sank,
    Rose other hearts above:
Bless her, dear sisters, bless and thank,
  For teaching how to love.
    He from his own had welcome sad—
    "Away with him," said they;
Yet never lord or poet had
  Such homage in his day.
    Ah Lord! in whose forgiveness sweet,
    Our life becomes intense!
We, brothers, sisters, crowd thy feet—
  Ah! make no difference.
    THE END.

Made in the USA
Lexington, KY
01 April 2014